The Sisters Club
Cloudy
with a
Chance of Boys

MEGAN McDONALD

CANDLEWICK PRESS

This is a work of fiction. Names, characters, places, and incidents are either products of the author's imagination or, if real, are used fictitiously.

First edition 2011

Library of Congress Cataloging-in-Publication Data is available.

Library of Congress Catalog Card Number 2010039179

ISBN 978-0-7636-4615-8

11 12 13 14 15 16 BVG 10 9 8 7 6 5 4 3 2 1

Printed in Berryville, VA, U.S.A.

This book was typeset in Cheltenham, Kidprint, and Passport.

Candlewick Press
99 Dover Street
Somerville, Massachusetts 02144

visit us at www.candlewick.com

For Andrea

Under the Mackerel Sky

I used to think weather was boring.

Something old people talk about to fill an empty room with conversation. Just look at my nana and papa—they're permanently tuned to the Weather Channel.

Weather was one of those things I never really paid attention to.

That was before.

Before the lights went out during the Storm of the Century. Before the frogs appeared. Before I got my first detention.

Before the tsunami.

But that comes later.

I guess you could say I have weather on the brain these days. We're doing a serious weather unit in Earth Science, and I am like a semi–cloud expert now. I've spent a lot of time watching clouds from the third-story attic window of our crooked old Victorian. Some days I climb up Reindeer Hill to observe clouds and look for unusual cloud shapes. Then, I take pictures to document them. I'm making a cloud chart, which is like a mega-poster filled with cool photos of all kinds of clouds — cumulus, cirrus, stratonimbus.

At first, it was just a school project I had to do to get a decent grade. But the more I watched, the more I began to think clouds have . . . personalities. One minute they look like happy puffs of cotton candy — marshmallow castles in the air. Then you blink, and right before your eyes that same cloud has morphed into a snake or a dragon.

Come to think of it, clouds are like sisters. I should know. I have two of them — Alex, my older sister, and Joey, who's two years younger than me.

Alex, I would have to say, is a thunderhead: dark and mysterious, quick to anger, as if there's a storm gathering inside her. Joey is a cumulus: a happy cloud that comes out on a bright, blue-sky day and looks like a bunny wearing fuzzy bedroom slippers.

Me, I'm more of a cirrostratus, what the science book calls "uniform clouds, hardly discernible, capable of forming halos." They look like light brushstrokes across the sky. You know, the even, steady kind. Always there, but sometimes you don't even notice.

I never thought much about clouds, really, till now. Suddenly, they're everywhere. In Shakespeare, Hamlet looks at clouds and compares them to a camel, then a weasel, not to mention a whale. In Language Arts, a poem we studied by e. e. cummings had a locomotive spouting violets, which I think must be clouds. There's even a local chapter of the Cloud Appreciation Society, right here in Acton, Oregon. They have a logo and everything.

But the most important thing about clouds is that they give you a hint about what's to come. All you have to do is see the signs. Read the sky.

Right after we started our weather unit, I noticed trees were leafing. Somewhere, frogs dreamed of hatching. Joey told me once that frogs can actually smell danger before they hatch. All I could smell was rain.

And then, for three days, we were under a mackerel sky—a sky filled with cirrocumulus and altocumulus clouds. Think buttermilk. Think thousands of tiny fish scales. A mackerel sky means three things: precipitation, instability, and *thunderstorms.*

So, for all I know about weather, you'd think I would have seen it coming. I should have known that something was about to happen. Something that would change me. Us. The sisters.

You can smell rain. You can hear thunder coming. But there's not a weatherman on the planet who could have given me this forecast: cloudy, with a chance of boys.

Change in the Weather

One minute we were just talking and being sisters. The next minute, we were in the dark.

Here's what happened. Alex, Medieval Fashion Designer, was stretched out on the floor, surrounded by twenty-seven thousand colored pencils scattered like Pick-up Sticks. She was designing a fancy costume for Juliet ("*Romeo's better half,*" she says) instead of drawing a self-portrait for Art class.

Joey was making animal sculptures out of colored marshmallows. She found an old cookbook of Mom's from the 1960s with marshmallow animals, and she's working on a whole zoo, complete with lions, elephants, and giraffes.

I was way into pasting pictures of clouds on a giant

three-fold poster board for Mr. Petry's Earth Science class.

"Since when did the Sisters Club become the Homework Club?" I asked.

Just then, a giant boom of thunder shook the house. Rain pelted the windows, rattling them in their frames. A crack of lightning lit the room with an eerie flash.

"Wow. It's a real weather freak show out there," I said.

The lights flickered. On-off. On-off-on.

Alex looked up from her sketchbook.

"Uh-oh," said Joey.

In a blink, the whole house went dark. We're talking pitch-black, can't-see-your-hand-in-front-of-you night.

Joey ran to get a flashlight, bouncing it off the walls like a light show. *Ahh!* She shined the light right in my face just to bug me.

"Okay, Duck," I said, holding up my arm to shield my face.

Mom burst through the door, smelling of pine and mud and bark. "Wind's really wicked out there," she said, plunking down an armload of wood, her wild hair studded with wet leaves.

"Mom. Hair," Alex pointed.

"You wouldn't believe all the branches that have come down," she said, pulling leaves from her hair. "Dad's trying to clear the sidewalk. Power could be out for a while. I'm going to build up the fire. The heat may not come back on right away, so we better keep the fire going."

"Just like Victorian times!" said Joey. Ever since Joey's *Little Women* phase, she thinks old-timey stuff is way cool. Me, I like my electricity. Not to mention soap.

Mom poked at the logs in the fireplace until the fire blazed bright orange.

The back door blew open. Dad came in and set a flashlight on the counter, shaking rain from his hair like a dog after a bath. "Phew. It's a real tempest out there." Dad's an actor and owns the Raven Theater next door. He's always spouting Shakespeare and stuff.

Dad dried his sleeves and warmed his hands in front of the fire. Wind whistled down the chimney.

"'Blow winds and crack your cheeks. Rage! Blow!' You know, girls, in Shakespeare, when there's a wild storm like this, like in *King Lear,* it means something big is about to happen."

"Yeah, like murder!" I said. Joey clutched my arm.

"The storm can't be all bad. Maybe something different and exciting is going to happen to us," said Dad.

"Dad, you're such a Drama Queen," said Alex.

"Look who's talking," I said.

"I love storms," said Joey.

"No, you love frogs," I said.

"Duh. After a storm, millions of frogs come out."

"Girls, help me with the candles," said Mom.

Alex helped Mom light tea candles inside tuna fish cans. Spooky shadows like wolves and flying birds flickered across the walls.

"Let's make hand shadows!" said Joey. "Like they did in Victorian times. I know how to make a swan." Joey formed a beak with one hand and made feathers with the other.

"Well," said Dad. "Time to go brave the elements again. A huge tree limb came down and fell across the back fence." He shrugged on his already dripping-wet coat and headed out the back door.

"So, are you girls okay for now? I'll check back in a while. I better help Dad with that branch if there's any hope of saving the fence."

"We're okay," I answered. "It's all good."

"Except for Alex stepped on my marshmallow giraffe," said Joey, shining the flashlight on her smushed creation. "Now he looks like a headless weasel."

"Did not," said Alex. "How do you know it wasn't Stevie?"

"Because," I said, "she can tell it was your big old teenager feet."

"Girls," said Mom. "I'm sure you can come up with something to do in the dark besides drive each other crazy. Stevie, keep the fire going, okay? And try to keep your sisters from squabbling." She headed out the back door after Dad.

"Me? Why's it always me?" I asked as soon as she was gone.

"Squabble, squabble," said Alex, making turkey gobbling sounds, and we couldn't help cracking up.

"Oh, well. I guess we'll just have to eat this one." Joey held up her headless weasel-giraffe with the broken neck.

"Ha. I don't think so! Not after you licked every one of them," said Alex.

"Not *every* one."

"What ever happened to Jell-O?" I asked. "I thought you lived for Jell-O."

"Jell-O's cool. But, it's just so third grade." Alex cracked up.

"Check it out! *Creck-eck. Creck-eck.*" Joey made a hand-shadow frog on the wall. "Well, if you guys aren't going to make hand shadows, let's do something scary since the lights are out. Like tell scary stories," she suggested.

A crack of thunder made Joey jump.

"You always want us to tell scary stories, Duck. Then you keep me up all night because you're too scared to go to sleep or you have bad dreams."

"We could have a séance," said Joey. "Maybe there's a ghost of a dead person who used to live in our house hundreds of years ago, and we could communicate with it."

"How do you know about séances?" Alex asked.

"Victorian times," Joey and I said at the exact same time.

"Jinx. You owe me a hot chocolate," I said, punching Joey in the arm.

"I know. How about fortune-telling?" said Alex. "I went to this girl Mira's fourteenth birthday party. Remember? It was a sleepover and we stayed up all night for the first time ever. Well, all except for this one girl, Alyssa."

"Mira? Alyssa? Who are they?" I asked.

"Just some girls I know. Anyway—the really cool part was Mira's mom hired this fortune-teller to read our palms. Check out my heart line." She pointed to a line that creased her palm like a half-moon. "The fortune-teller said it means I'm very lovable."

I peered at my palm in the candlelight. A map of glue was stuck to my hand. "What does it mean if your heart line is covered in glue?"

"It means you're *stuck* up," said Alex.

"Ha, ha. Very funny."

"You guys," said Joey. "Let's roast marshmallows in the fire. Please? I have pink, blue, and green marshmallows. We can make rainbow s'mores!"

I was only half listening. I stared at the fire, hypnotized, peeling glue off my palm as if shedding an old skin. A small yellow flame licked the edges of a piece of kindling, then burst into a blaze. Orange fingers of fire flickered and danced, casting a spell on me.

Alex's excited voice broke into my far-off daydream. "I got it, you guys," said Alex. "I know what we can do. It's perfect."

"What?" Joey and I said at the same time again. But by the time I'd gotten done jinxing her, Alex had left and gone upstairs.

Marshmallow Fun Facts

by Joey Reel

Ancient Egyptians invented marshmallows four thousand years ago. Only gods, kings, and queens were allowed to eat them. They got them from the mallow plant, which grows wild in marshes. Get it? Marsh mallow.

Alex can eat marshmallows since she's a Drama QUEEN. ~S

Oh, like you're so "mallow." Ha, ha! A.

In the U.S., people buy 90 million pounds of marshmallows every year. This equals the weight of 1,286 gray whales!

The marshmallow capital of the world is Acton, Oregon. Not! It's Ligonier, Indiana.

The largest s'more ever made weighed 1,600 pounds! It was made of 20,000 marshmallows and 7,000 chocolate bars and 24,000 graham crackers. Yum!

If you name your pet Marshmallow, that's a number 9 in numerology. Nine means your pet will be loyal and faithful to you. Huh? ~S

It's true. I read it in a magazine. They match a number to your pet's name. A.

What if you named a frog Macbeth? —J

Seven years BAD luck! A.

Rainbow S'mores
by Joey Reel

with help from me ~S

You will need:

- Graham crackers
- Colored marshmallows
- Chocolate bars

1. Put one large colored marshmallow on the end of a long fork or stick. Hold over campfire or in fireplace until toasted.
2. Break graham cracker in half and put piece of chocolate on it.
3. Smush ooey-gooey marshmallow on top of chocolate.
4. Use other half of graham cracker for a lid, like a marshmallow sandwich.
5. Don't forget to say you want 'some more'! Yum!

HINT: Mix it up a little and add peanut butter! Or chocolate icing!

Try frozen s'mores. Use ice cream instead of marshmallows. ~S

Stevie's chocolate chip cookies work too, in place of graham crackers. Decadent! A.

OOEY GOOEY

Something Witchy This Way Comes

Alex came back waving one of her teen magazines at us and carrying a small box. Her eyes looked even greener than usual in the eerie glow of the flashlight.

"We don't have to take one of your quizzes, do we?" I asked, trying to dig a splinter from my finger in the firelight.

"Some quizzes are cool," said Joey.

"No, not a quiz. It's this thing we were going to do at the sleepover, but you have to have a real fire. So tonight is perfect."

I felt a shiver. The hairs on my arms stood up. This was going to be good.

"Joey, hold the flashlight. Okay, it's right here on page fifty-seven," said Alex, squinting to see.

Joey looked over her shoulder and read the headline. "*How to Get Noticed by a Boy*?" She said it like a question. "No way!" she protested. "I'm not putting gunk on my face. And I'm not putting curlers in my hair. And I'm definitely not brushing on any shadows to make my nose look smaller, because—guess what?—not every girl in the world has nose envy!"

"Chill out, Stressarella. No makeup. Honest." Alex held up her hand like she was taking a solemn oath. "It's cool. See, you follow the directions, it tells you right here—"

"But Stevie and I don't care about boys, do we, Stevie?" Joey gave me a look that pleaded, *Back me up, here.*

I looked down at my palm. I didn't answer. I went back to working on the splinter in my finger. It's not like I'm boy crazy or anything—not like Olivia and half the girls in my grade. But I *was* a little curious to hear what Alex had to say.

"It doesn't have to be about boys," said Alex. "It can be about anything. It's just a way to make something happen that you want to come true. Like a wish," she said to Joey.

"You mean like a magic spell?" asked Joey.

"Um . . . sure," said Alex. "It'll be like the three witches in *Macbeth*."

"Can't we just wish on a wishbone like normal people?" said Joey.

"BORing," said Alex, imitating Joey.

"Okay, but I'm only doing it if we get to say 'eye of newt' and stuff," Joey said.

"Sure!" said Alex. "Then we get to throw stuff in the fire! It'll be cool, right, Stevie?"

"I guess," I said. There had been a momentary calm, but now the angry storm was picking up outside again. "As long as we don't have to burn our fingernail clippings or anything creepy like that. And you're not getting a lock of my hair, or my baby tooth. And no blood. And definitely no dancing around in our underwear!"

"Same here," said Joey. "All that stuff Stevie said."

"Nothing like that, you guys. But I do have some incense we can burn. Winterforest Dewberry or Cherry Manlove?"

"Is that really what they're called?" I asked, taking

the box from Alex and holding it up to my nose. "Uck. They *both* smell like wet dog hair."

"Cherry, cherry, cherry, cherry, cherry," Joey chanted. I guess she didn't hear the "manlove" part.

"Cherry it is," said Alex. "And we already have candles and a fire."

When had my sister the Drama Queen turned into a Pyro Queen? Alex Reel, Pyromaniac, at your service.

"Step one. First we have to close our eyes and take three deep breaths," Alex instructed us. "Concentrate. Focus. Think of something you want to happen. Then picture it in your mind's eye."

I closed my eyes. Something I would like to happen? *Have an extra-cheese pizza appear before me. Get an A on my Earth Science project. Not have to clean my room.*

"Can it be something we *don't* want to happen?" I asked.

"Shh," said Alex.

If I had one wish, what would it be? To have the lights come back on so I don't have to do this? I wish . . . I wish . . . why can't I think of anything to wish? I wish my hair would grow . . . Lame-o. Think, Stevie, think.

A low rumble of thunder sent a chill through me, raising the hair on my arms. "Open your eyes," said Alex in a spooky voice. She read from the magazine again. "Step two. Keeping the person in mind, think of an object related to that person. Choose something close to your heart that has special meaning. Step three. Say the magic words, close your eyes, and toss your Special Object into the fire."

"Person? What person?" Joey asked. "You mean a boy? You said it wasn't about boys. You so lie."

"It just means—never mind. I forgot we're not doing the boy thing. So think of the *thing* you wish to happen, and pick an object to throw in the fire. But it has to be something you like a lot. Something personal. Something that's hard to give up. Otherwise it won't work."

"Says who?"

"Says step number three, right here." Alex jabbed the magazine with her finger. "You guys take the other flashlight. Let's go find our good luck charms."

"But I don't have a wish!" I called after Alex, but she was already headed for the stairs.

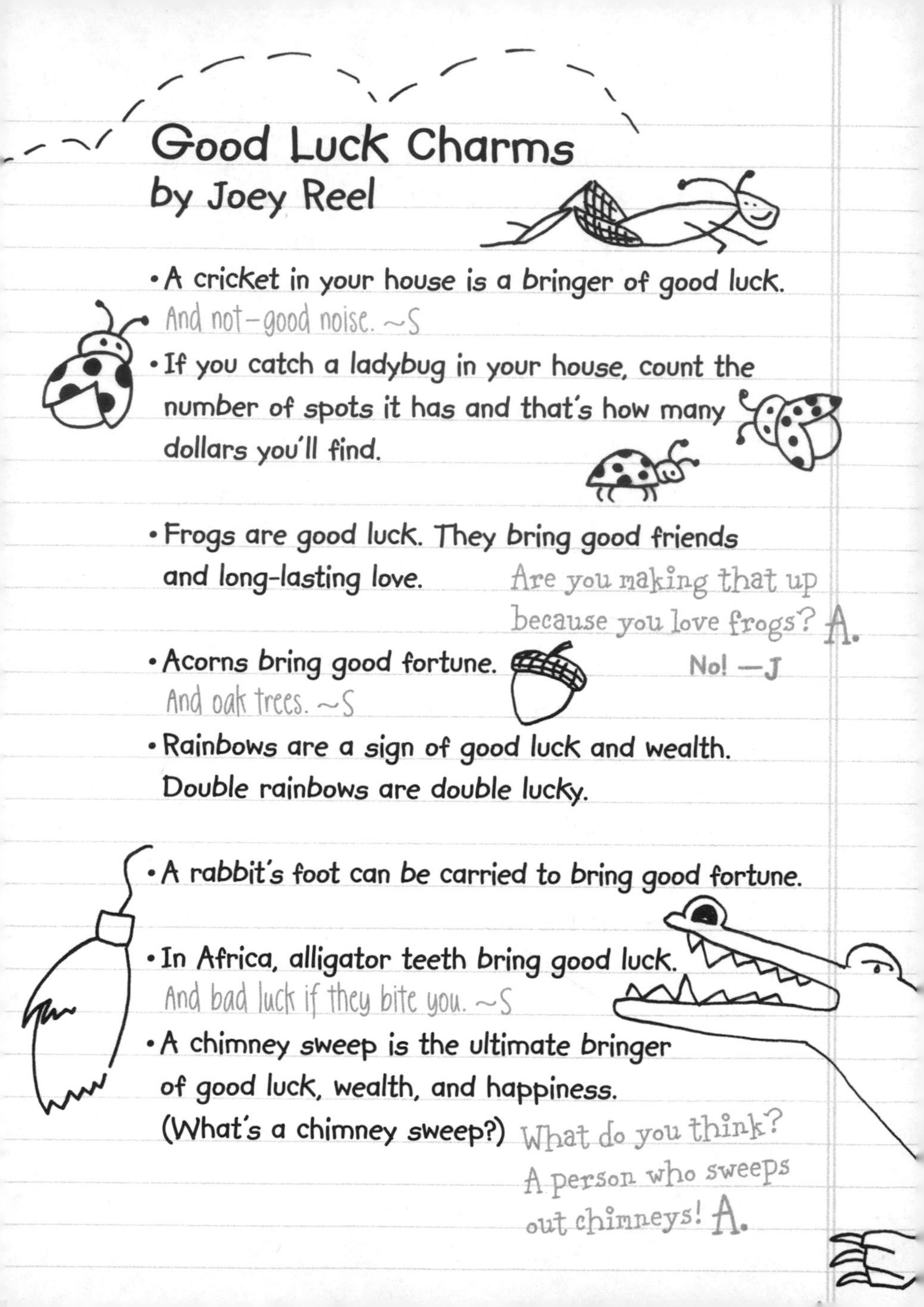

Good Luck Charms
by Joey Reel

- A cricket in your house is a bringer of good luck.

And not-good noise. ~S

- If you catch a ladybug in your house, count the number of spots it has and that's how many dollars you'll find.

- Frogs are good luck. They bring good friends and long-lasting love.

Are you making that up because you love frogs? A.

No! —J

- Acorns bring good fortune.

And oak trees. ~S

- Rainbows are a sign of good luck and wealth. Double rainbows are double lucky.

- A rabbit's foot can be carried to bring good fortune.

- In Africa, alligator teeth bring good luck.

And bad luck if they bite you. ~S

- A chimney sweep is the ultimate bringer of good luck, wealth, and happiness. (What's a chimney sweep?)

What do you think? A person who sweeps out chimneys! A.

- If you rub a Buddha's belly, you'll have good luck. Good luck finding a Buddha. ~S
- See a penny, pick it up, and all day you'll have good luck. Or carry a penny with your birth year for luck.
- A horseshoe pointing up means good luck.
- The number 7 is way lucky.
- Four-leaf clovers are the luckiest!
- A shooting star is lucky and means you get to make a wish. A wishbone or an eyelash works too.
- A key is one of the oldest good luck charms.

Yeah, it brings good luck opening the door. A.

If Wishes Were Trolls . . .

Joey and I climbed the stairs behind Alex. Alex went straight to her room and came back with an old shoebox full of baby stuff and mementos. In no time, Joey was ready too.

But I bounced the beam around our room, looking for something, anything, to throw into the fire. An old journal, a cooking contest ribbon, a cupcake candle I got in my Christmas stocking? School picture? A picture of Act Two, our old dog? My last report card? Friendship bracelet from Olivia? It was kind of hard to choose, since I really didn't know what to wish.

In the distance, I could hear an emergency siren.

Then, in the beam of my flashlight, I caught sight of

a troll doll with neon-green hair and a diamond in its belly, giving me the evil eye.

Perfect! Mom once told me that trolls were supposed to be good luck. I grabbed the troll doll by its green hair. Who didn't want to wish for good luck?

We crept back downstairs and all three of us crouched in front of the fire.

"Alex, what did you pick?" Joey asked eagerly.

"Um . . . it's a secret," said Alex. "You're not supposed to tell, or show your Special Object to anybody. Keep it in your pocket or behind your back till we're ready."

"What magic words should we say?" Joey asked.

"How about if I say the 'Double, double, toil and trouble' part, then you guys answer, 'By the pricking of my thumbs / Something wicked this way comes.'"

Branches scratched against the window like fingernails on a chalkboard. I felt a shiver up my back.

"Too creepy," Joey said.

"Okay . . ." said Alex, in a thin voice. "How about, 'Come you spirits, make my blood thick—'"

"No blood!" I reminded Alex.

"C'mon, you guys. You're wrecking the mood."

"Yeah, Joey, stop wrecking the mood," I teased. I wiggled my troll doll in her face to spook her.

"Hey, she showed us her Special Object. You're not supposed to show us your Special Object," said Joey. "Do you think the magic will still work, Alex?"

"It'll work," Alex said. "Okay, you guys. Be serious. This is it. Close your eyes. I'm going to say something in Shakespeare, and you can't fight me on it. Then I'll count to three. On the count of three, open your eyes, and we each toss our Special Objects into the fire at the same time. Ready? Remember, the most important part is you have to *believe*."

I closed my eyes. The darkness heightened every sound—wind whipping through the trees outside, the ticking of the old mantel clock, my sisters' breathing. My own heart thumping.

That's when I knew I wanted to wish for something besides just ordinary good luck. It was probably just hocus-pocus, but somehow—call it the storm, the dark, the firelight—this felt bigger than a birthday-candle wish.

I'd wish for . . . something new and exciting to happen to me. Something different. Something daring.

Like when I tried out to be in the musical *Once Upon a Mattress.* Or entered a Cupcake Cooking Contest.

Alex made her voice soft and spooky again. "'Stars, hide your fires! Let not light see my black and deep desires.'"

Thunk! "What was that?" I asked.

"Just a branch hitting the roof," said Alex.

I opened one eye and peeked. A reflection of firelight flickered in the troll doll's eyes. Alex was holding a play program from *Beauty and the Beast,* and Joey had an origami frog in her hand.

"One . . . two . . . three . . ." *Boom!* A loud crack of thunder shook the house just as we opened our eyes and tossed our Special Objects into the fire. I jumped. Joey screamed and grabbed onto Alex. A streak of lightning flashed blue and the fire flared up. Tongues of flame licked the edges of Alex's program and *poof,* it disappeared into ash. Joey's frog went up in smoke. The troll doll melted quicker than the Wicked Witch.

All of a sudden, a string of pearl-size goose bumps ran up and down my spine. A thrilling kind of tickle at the base of my neck needled me. I scratched it, as if touching it might make it go away.

Maybe it was just the dark, the night, the storm. The gleam in my sister's eye. What was Alex playing at? Wasn't this just a game? What if we had done something, started something, called on something—unleashed something invisible, something bigger than us, this room, this night?

"Joey, I thought that was your favorite origami frog," I said to break the spell. "The one you got to jump the best."

"Hey! You weren't supposed to see," said Joey.

"It doesn't matter. We all know anyway," I said.

"Nuh-uh," said Joey. "Nobody knows what Alex threw in the fire."

"But we all know what she wished for," I said.

Alex's head snapped around to glare at me. "What?"

"To get the part of Juliet in the play. Duh. What else?"

"Oh," said Alex. "Yeah." She laughed a nervous laugh, but something secret and shadowy passed over those Mona Lisa eyes of hers. "*Look like the innocent flower/But be the serpent under it,*" I thought as another line from *Macbeth* sprang to mind.

I'd have to wait and see if something new and exciting happened to me. Time would tell. I guess the most I could hope for was that the spell didn't turn my hair neon green and make it stand up as straight as a troll's.

One glass troll eye stared at me from the bottom of the fireplace. Part of me wanted to yell *Wait!* and take it back. But it was too late.

A last line from *Macbeth* niggled the back of my brain.

"What's done is done."

I, the GREAT SOCK MONKEY SWAMI

Did you know your hand tells a story?
What does it say about YOU?

HOW FRIENDLY ARE YOU? IS LOVE COMING YOUR WAY?
Take a look at your heart line.

- **Unbroken line:** You form deep friendships. When you love someone, they are certain to love you back.
- **Lines crossing heart line:** Your love life will have ups and downs.

ARE YOU A BRAINIAC? A THINKER? AN ARTIST?
Check out your head line.

- **Straight line:** You are brainy and a strong thinker.
- **Slight curve:** You are creative and artistic. Pick up that pen, pencil, or paintbrush!
- **Downward turn:** You are an independent thinker. You think outside the box.

WHAT DOES YOUR FUTURE HOLD?
Your fate line will reveal all!

- **Strong, unbroken line:** Success will come easy to you!
- **Broken line:** Be ready for obstacles and disappointments along the way.

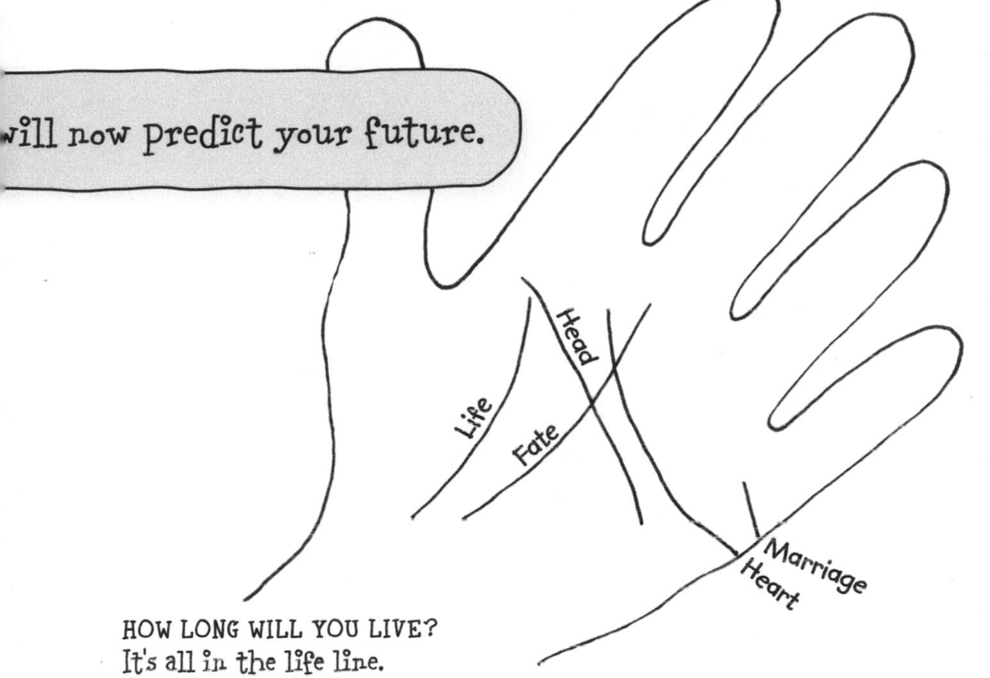
will now predict your future.
Head
Life
Fate
Marriage
Heart

HOW LONG WILL YOU LIVE?

It's all in the life line.

- **Long, unbroken line:** You will live a long, healthy life.
- **Broken line:** Take good care of yourself. You may have some health challenges.

WILL YOU MARRY? HOW MANY KIDS WILL YOU HAVE?

Easy-peasy. Look for the marriage line.

- **Number of lines:** These indicate how many times you will get married.
- **Number of lines that touch the marriage line:** these indicate how many kids you will have!

LOOK FOR THESE SHAPES ON YOUR PALM:

Square: You are protected and safe. **Triangle:** Beware!

Broken line: You will have a setback.

Cross: Trouble is near. **Star:** You are coming into money.

Grid: You are stressed out. Relax!

Frog Encounters of the First Kind
by Joey Reel

Frogs! It's raining frogs! Not really — but millions of them did come out after the big storm. They hop all over the road, and at night you see them hopping in the headlights of cars. Sounds like a giant tree frog sleepover!

Q: When is a tree frog not a tree frog?
A: When it's a Pacific tree frog! (They don't live in trees but don't ask me why.)

Pacific tree frogs can change colors, too! They can morph from brown to green or from spots to plain! Their color depends on the light, how wet it is, and their mood! Some tree frogs are missing their yellow color, so even though they're really green, without the yellow color in there, they look blue!

I'm dying to see a blue frog!
(That was my wish! Shh!
It's a secret.)

- Number of frogs hopping in the street after the storm: 10 gazillion!
- Number of sisters trying to catch frogs: 3 minus Alex = 2
- Number of frogs caught by Joey: 7
- Number of frogs caught by Stevie: 11 (she says)
- Number of frogs <u>really</u> caught by Stevie: 3
- Number of frogs Stevie will let me keep: 0
- Number of frogs I'm going to keep anyway: 1
  — Shh! Don't tell Stevie!
  (P.S. I named him Sir Croaks-a-Lot)
- Number of blue frogs I found: 0
- Number of blue frogs I hope to see someday: 2
  (Blue poison arrow frog and blue Pacific tree frog)

FIRST KISS WISH
Starring Alex

Sock Monkey: So, you're still talking to me, huh?

Me: Why wouldn't I be?

Sock Monkey: It's just . . . you hardly ever have time for me anymore.

Me: You sound like my sisters. Of course I haven't forgotten you. Who else am I going to tell my secrets to? *Not* the Snoopy Sisters, that's for sure.

Sock Monkey: The Snoopy Sisters. Good one.

Me: So, do you want to know my secret or what?

Sock Monkey: I'm all ears! Even though I don't have ears. Why don't you give me some ears?

Me: You had ears once upon a time. But they got all loved off.

Sock Monkey: Aw.

Me: Okay, listen up. Remember a couple of nights ago, during the blackout, when I—

Sock Monkey: Did a magic *love* spell? Yeah, I remember. You went to all that trouble, when you could just write down the person's name and put it under your pillow. Or eat three petals of the black jade rose while thinking of the person's name.

Me: Can we focus here? Unless you don't want to know my secret.

Sock Monkey: Like I said, I'm all ears.

Me: Okay. So. You know how I threw that note from when I was in *Beauty and the Beast* with Scott Howell in the fire that night?

Sock Monkey: Yeah, that was really using your brain. Now you burned up his love note and you don't have it anymore.

Me: It wasn't a love note anyway. I wish. It just said, *"See you at practice. S."* No biggie.

Sock Monkey: Uh-huh. So, why'd you save that play program forever?

Me: I know Stevie and Joey think I wished

that I'd get to play Juliet in the school play, but really I wished—

Sock Monkey: For secret crush Scott Towel to like you?

Me: A) His name is not Scott Towel! It's Scott Howell. That's just what my annoying sisters call him. And B) I wished for something better than that. *Way* better.

Sock Monkey: What? That'd he'd call you up? Send you a *real* love note? Ask you out to a vampire movie?

Me: Nope, nope, and nope.

Sock Monkey: That he'd come over for dinner again, and this time not drop his fork in the fondue and have to kiss everybody at the table?

Me: Wrong again.

Sock Monkey: What? I give up. Tell me!

Me: Okay, but you have to keep it a secret. Nobody but you in the whole entire world can know. Are you ready?

Sock Monkey: Hurry up! Whisper it in my

ear. I mean, where my ear would be if I had one.

Me: I wished that I would get my first kiss, and it would be from *him.*

Sock Monkey: Who him?

Me: *Him,* him. Romeo.

Sock Monkey: Huh?

Me: Don't you get it? I have it all planned. I get the part of Juliet in the play, and Scott is Romeo. And Romeo has to kiss Juliet, right? So, voila! I get my first kiss. What could be better than a sweet, romantic, Romeo-and-Juliet kind of first kiss?

Sock Monkey: Brilliant!

Me: I thought so. Now all I need is to really rock my audition, get the part of Juliet, hope Scott gets the part of Romeo, and convince Mr. Cannon that you can't do *Romeo and Juliet* without at least one kissing scene.

Sock Monkey: Details, details.

Cloudy with a Chance of Boring

I glanced up at the clock on the wall — 1:29 and the crowds are getting restless.

No wonder. We've spent the last twenty-nine minutes smushed like sardines on the bleachers with hundreds of antsy sixth graders and rowdy seventh graders in the multipurpose room, waiting for the assembly to start.

Olivia and I have been through our share of Author Day assemblies together. Once, back in kindergarten, this grumpy teacher yelled at me for telling the Author a story about putting a rubber ear in Joey's spaghetti (that joke never gets old), and Livvie stood up for me and said it was a funny story. We've been best friends ever since.

"Who's the author supposed to be, anyway?" I asked Liv.

"You know it'll be some guy who tells seriously lame jokes."

Afternoon forecast: Cloudy with a chance of boring.

"Or some guy whose great-great-great-great-grandfather walked the Oregon Trail," said some kid behind us, butting into our conversation.

I mouthed, *"Who's he?"* to Olivia. She shrugged.

The kid's knee bumped me in the back of the head.

"Hey!" I said, turning around to squinch my face at him. He had short sandy blond hair and wire-rimmed glasses that looked kind of cool and ungeeky. And he was wearing a black T-shirt with Oscar the Grouch peeking out of a garbage can. Go figure. I never get the shirts guys wear.

"Sorry. My bad. I, um, it's my second day here. I was at East, then we moved, like, 1.4 miles, and they transferred me to West."

"Interesting," I said. *"Not!"* I mouthed to Olivia, and she started giggling.

"Hey, I mean, aren't you in my Earth Science class?" he asked.

"Me? No," said Olivia, shaking her head.

He was looking at me. "I don't know. Am I?" I said.

"Yeah. With that guy. What's his name? Mr. Petri Dish."

Olivia and I couldn't help laughing a little. "Mr. Petry. Minus the dish. Um, word of advice? You better not let him hear you calling him that, or you'll be staying after to wash all his Petri dishes till they sparkle."

Ms. Carter-Dunne leaned forward from her seat at the end of the row and put a finger to her lips to shush us.

The assistant principal was yammering on about something. I'm not into being a rowdy sixth grader, but I am into telling Olivia the whole story about the storm and the power outage and the Sisters Club with the you-know-what in the fire and hoping my hair would not turn green.

"Speaking of green," I said, "did I mention I have a new roommate? Joey adopted a frog. After the storm. She doesn't know I know."

"Wait," said Olivia, "so now you have a frog living in your room? For real?"

"Frog? Who lives with a frog?" Wire Rims asked Olivia.

"Don't you know it's rude to listen in on other people's conversations?" Olivia said.

"Sorry. Couldn't help overhearing."

She turned back to me. "Where were we? Oh, yeah. You were burning a troll doll and wishing for stuff and—"

Ms. Carter-Dunne glared at us.

"Shh! Stop saying troll doll," I warned, making fierce eyes at Olivia.

"Did you guys say Roald Dahl? Is that who the author is? For real?"

"Yeah, that's who it is. Except for one teeny-weeny detail. Roald Dahl is dead!" Olivia told him.

"Too bad," I joked. "I love his book *James and the Giant* Eavesdropper." Olivia and I cracked up.

Just then, the principal came out and tapped on the microphone. He cleared his throat and the room settled down to a dull roar. Behind him stood a guy with greased-back hair, wearing a black-and-white suit.

"Boys and girls," the principal started, and Olivia whispered, "Uh-oh, bad news." Whenever the principal starts out with "Boys and girls," it's bad news.

"I know you've all been looking forward to Author Day *(we have?)* and you've been preparing for this day in your classes *(huh?)* but I'm sorry to have to announce that our author is . . . has a bad case of . . . stomach flu—"

Wire Rims whispered, "Stomach flu, huh? That's code talk for you-know-what. Hey, maybe he's the author of *The Princess Diarrheas.* Or *The Diarrhea of Anne Frank.*"

"That is *so* not funny," Olivia told him, but we couldn't help laughing a little.

"*Diarrhea of a Wimpy Kid,*" he said, trying too hard to get us to crack up some more. I glanced over at Ms. Carter-Dunne, but luckily she was giving the evil eye to Ben Cheng.

"But the good news is that we had an assembly scheduled for the primary classes and our speaker has agreed to stay to address the sixth and seventh graders. Let me introduce the Nutrition Magician!" Collective crowd groan.

"Nutrition Magician?" Wire Rims leaned in and said to Olivia, "Suddenly, the dead author's not looking so bad, am I right?"

"Shh! Don't you know how to whisper?" Olivia nodded toward the teacher.

The Nutrition Magician pulled a zucchini out of a black top hat. Nobody laughed. Before you could say "Food Pyramid," he started juggling the major food groups—two eggplants, an orange, a carton of milk, and a rolling pin.

Just then, I felt a knee in the back of my head again. "Hey! You're pulling my hair! Ouch!"

He said, "Sorry," but he was clearly grinning.

"You don't look sorry," said Olivia. She was grinning too.

The Nutrition Magician dropped the rolling pin by mistake. The audience erupted in laughter.

"So, you're in her Earth Science class?" Olivia asked Wire Rims. "What's your name, again?"

"Owen. Owen O'Malley. But my friends call me Owen." He smacked his hand on his forehead like he didn't mean to say that.

"Really? Strange. My name's Stevie but my friends call me Stevie." I couldn't help grinning.

When the assembly was over, we got the nods from our teachers that it was time to go back to class.

"Finally. I've never heard so many questions about broccoli," Olivia said.

"That's because nobody wants to go back to class." Including me. The assembly had been kind of fun. Missing Health class, I mean. And talking to Livvie the whole time.

As we filed past Ms. Carter-Dunne, I smiled. She did not smile back. She frowned and pointed to Olivia, me, and Wire Rims. "You, you, and you. Wait for me out in the hall. Now."

SEALED WITH A KISS
Starring Alex

Sisters Stevie and Joey enter room, interrupting my perfect scene.

Me: *But soft! What light through yonder window breaks?*
It is the East, and Juliet is the sun!
Arise, fair sun, and kill the envious moon
Who is already sick and pale with grief.

Joey: Here we go again. Alex is being Juliet. That means we're supposed to be quiet.

Stevie: Another death scene? Alex, you have more lives than a cat!

Me: *(Holds up black eye mask on stick and waves it in front of sisters.)* I'm not Juliet. I'm Romeo. And it's not a death scene; it's a love scene.

Joey: Ooh. Ick.

Stevie: My bad.

Joey: Are you sure? Because you're flinging

your head back and grabbing your heart. And that's what you usually do when you're stabbed or poisoned.

Me: I'm sure. It's the balcony scene from *Romeo and Juliet*. The balcony scene is only one of the greatest love scenes of all time! Ask anybody—dying and falling in love are the two hardest things an actor will ever have to do.

Joey: Does Romeo wear a mask, like a robber?

Me: Duh. Romeo meets Juliet at a masked ball. He has to go in disguise because Juliet's family hates him.

Joey: How come?

Me: Well, they don't just hate him, they hate his whole family. The Montagues and Capulets have been mortal enemies for, like, a million years. They hate him so bad they'll kill him on sight if they see him at the ball.

Joey: Wait a minute. I know this story. One's a Montague and one's a Capulet and they're madly in love, and they rub noses a lot, but their moms and dads are super mad at them. They keep trying to get Juliet to marry this other guy, who's really big and has bad breath that makes her cough all the time. He's a walrus, I think. Or an elephant seal.

Stevie: *(Laughs.)* A *walrus*?

Joey: Yeah. *(Shrugs.)* I saw the cartoon. Romeo and Juliet are seals, and there's this talking fish named Kissy who's really annoying. He sings "Twinkle, Twinkle, Little Star." Who sings "Twinkle, Twinkle" in the play?

Me: C'mon, you guys. You have to help me figure out what to do for the audition.

Joey: Sing "Twinkle, Twinkle, Little Star"!

Me: I mean, what should I do with my hair? *(Tugs on short hair.)*

Joey: How come nobody ever listens to me?

Stevie: Your hair's fine.

Me: My hair *was* fine, until *somebody*

burned it with the iron and I had to get it all cut off!

Stevie: Well, you're the one who wanted straight hair. You forced me to iron your hair. I'm on record for saying it was a bad idea from the get-go. Ask Joey.

Joey: Me? Don't look at me. I wasn't even there!

Me: *(Makes face at Stevie.)*

Stevie: Okay, okay. Let's not even go there.

Me: You know, when you think about the Hair Ironing Disaster of the Century, you kinda owe me. So, I was thinking . . . I really need a Romeo. To practice for Juliet. *(Looks pleadingly at Stevie.)*

Stevie: Don't look at me! I'm not going to kiss you then drink poison or stab myself or whatever.

Me: It's the balcony scene. There's no poison. Romeo climbs up over the orchard wall to talk to Juliet.

Joey: *(Jokingly.)* Oh, Romeo, Romeo, I love you so much. Smooch, smooch, smooch.

(Makes kissing sounds on her arm.) You're my one and only lovey-dovey love bug. Oh Romeo, I just can't live without you. *(Mimes sticking finger down throat.)* Gag me with a spoon!

Me: Make fun all you want. But the part of Juliet is like a once-in-a-lifetime chance. Every actress has to play Juliet at least once.

Stevie: Especially if . . . I mean . . . you know who would make a great Romeo?

Joey: Scott Towel!

Me: *(Blushes.)*

Stevie: I was going to say Allen. Allen Albertson.

Me: Alvin the Chipmunk? Are you bonkers? That kid has see-through ears and more zits than there are craters on Saturn.

Joey: Ouch!

Stevie: *(Teasingly.)* But if he gets the part, you still want to be Juliet, right? I mean, as an actress. You'd still kiss him, I mean, for your career and everything.

Me: *(Shudders.)* He's not going to get the part.

Stevie: And Scott Towel is?

Me: The kiss has to be good. No, not good, off-the-charts great. Because it's her first kiss. And first kisses have to be perfect. *(Shuts eyes, imagining.)* For the play, I mean. *(Clears throat.)* To be believable. You know.

Joey: Juliet Capulet is kind of a weird name.

Stevie: How do you know it's her first kiss? Do they say it's her first kiss?

Me: I don't know. But she's only, like, thirteen in the play. Almost fourteen.

Joey: Your age.

Me: Exactly.

Joey: Blech. Forget about all that kissing. Just do what the seals do in the movie. *(Flaps hands together.) Arr! Arr! Arr! (Barks like a seal.)*

Stevie: *(Smacks hand to head.)* Wait a second. I get it. I see what this is all about now. You go out for Juliet and Scott Towel goes out for Romeo and Romeo kisses Juliet in the play so you get your first kiss from Romeo. I mean, Scott Towel!

Me: So?

Stevie: Aha! I was right.

Joey: Can we please stop talking about kissing? It's gross!

Me: What's gross about it?

Joey: Um, hello! There's spit involved, in case you hadn't noticed. And germs! Tons of germs. And pizza breath. And sometimes the guy sneezes on you.

Stevie: And braces. Don't forget braces. Total lip lock.

Me: Thou speaketh of such matters which thou haveth not a clue.

Stevie: Don't thou meaneth "clue-eth"?

A Hair-raising Adventure
by Joey Reel

Alex's hair got ironed off so she cut it super short. I donated mine to Locks of Love. And Stevie felt bad for us so she cut hers. Now Alex and Stevie want their hair to hurry up and grow.

A normal person has 100,000 strands of hair.

Once hair comes out of your scalp, it's actually dead!

Hair grows only about half an inch in a month.

When your hair hits your shoulder, that hair is about two years old.

Alex wants long hair to play Juliet. The play is in six weeks. That's not even one inch in hair time.

Stevie and I have, like, 5. A.

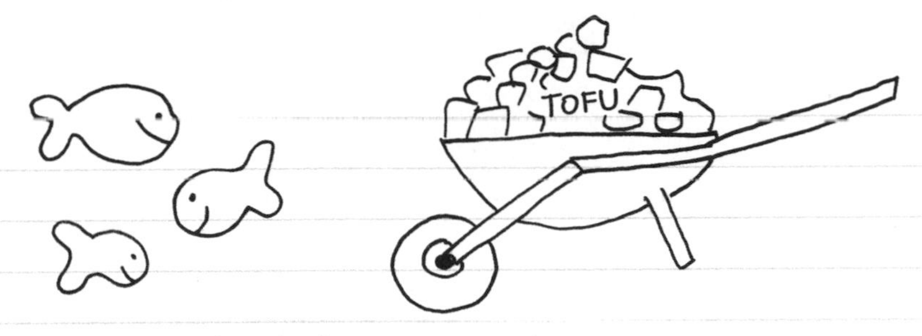

Tips for growing hair super fast:

- Eat fish. No way! ~S
- Eat eggs.
- Eat beans. No way! A.
- Eat yogurt.
- Eat tons of tofu! NO WAY! A. + S
- Eat calves liver. Reason to become instant vegetarian. A.
- Take vitamin B-6, zinc, and magnesium.
- Eat right & exercise. Huh? ~S
- Get lots of sleep.

I'm a teenager. Don't I always? A.

Reason to stop complaining about short hair. ~S

If all else fails:

- Get hair extensions, buy a clip-on ponytail, or wear a wig!

Cloudspotting

After leaving Alex's room, I felt all jumpy inside. Not sure why. Maybe it was the thought of telling Mom and Dad I got detention for talking during the assembly. It's not like it was Bad Kids Detention — I just had to stay after class in Ms. Carter-Dunne's homeroom with Olivia and Wire Rims. But still.

I plopped down on my bed, holding my head in my hands.

"What's the matter with you?" Joey asked.

"Frogs, for one thing. They're making my head hurt. Ever since the storm, they sound louder than ever. It sounds like we have a frog right in this room!"

"Um," Joey said. "I might have something to tell you."

"I know."

She reached into a tank under her bed and held out a bright green little frog with masked eyes. "Meet Sir Croaks-a-Lot."

"He is cute," I admitted.

"So I can I keep him in our room for a little while? I'll let him go, I promise. As soon as he gets better. He's missing two toes."

"We'll see. You'll have to ask Mom and Dad, you know." It wasn't Joey, or the frog—I just had to get out of there. I grabbed my camera and yanked a hoodie over my head.

"Where're you going?" Joey asked with a take-me-with-you sad-puppy look on her face.

"Cloudspotting."

"Cloud spitting? Sounds weird," Joey said.

"Cloud*spotting*. It's like those people in England who like to watch trains, only instead of trains, I'm going to watch clouds. It's for Earth Science. You know, my big poster board, where I have to document all different types of clouds? I thought I might find some unusual ones, now that the storm is over."

Joey grabbed her slicker off the hook in the front

hallway. "Hurry up," I said impatiently. "Before all the clouds blow away."

We stepped out under a sky full of patchy clouds, but the sun was starting to break through. Joey and I headed down the sidewalk toward Three Sisters Park, dodging puddles and climbing over branches knocked down from the storm. By the time we got to the top of Reindeer Hill, I was out of breath and my heart was pounding.

I stretched out on my back, crossed my feet, and folded my hands behind my head, staring up at the blue.

Joey and I lay there for a long time, watching the sky, not saying a word. I could feel the dampness through my shirt, smell the clean air. Something I like about Joey is that she's okay with being quiet. For some reason—the blue sky, the puffy clouds, the damp earth beneath my back—I felt like a little kid again.

"Look!" I said to Joey, pointing up. "I see a chicken."

Joey laughed. "That's a turkey." She tilted her head. "Or is it a dinosaur?"

The clouds were like shifting wisps of smoke, changing right above our heads. "Now I see a flying turtle." *Click. Click.* "No, wait. It's a giant hand."

"Sorry to tell you, but your giant hand is a fish with one fin."

"Do you see a dragon now?" I asked.

"No, but I see a dragon*fly*," she said. *Click, click.*

"Looks more like corkscrew pasta to me," I told her.

"Only someone who likes to cook as much as you would see a kind of noodle in the sky." Joey giggled. She moved her head sideways, looking at the cloud from different angles. "The dragonfly looks kind of like a frog on skis."

"I wondered how long it would take you to see a frog," I said, snapping a bunch more shots.

"Who knew there were so many different kinds of clouds? Now I see the state of Minnesota, a giant letter *H,* and a hyphen."

"A hyphen? Duck, only you would find punctuation in a cloud," I said, and Joey cracked up. "Do you think you're going to be a writer when you grow up?"

"Um-m-mm," Joey said, shrugging her shoulders. "How should I know?"

"Well, I definitely see you as a writer. A writer who uses lots of hyphens. In Minnesota." Joey grinned, and her two front teeth stuck out.

We stretched out side by side. I could hear the

wind in the leaves and my own breath. It felt good to do nothing but watch clouds.

"Hey, we should start calling you Zoey," I said out of the blue.

Joey leaned up and looked over at me, squinting. "Why?"

"I don't know. Why not? Because Zoey sounds like a writer's name. Because I'm feeling . . . I don't know . . . wild and weird and wonderful today, I think, I mean, I don't know *what* I'm feeling, actually."

Joey bolted up. "Okay, now you're starting to freak me out because you sound like Alex. The not-making-sense part, I mean."

"Don't worry, Duck. I'm still me," I assured her. But inside I felt like a different me. All fluttery and heart-skippy and breathless.

"So you're not going to stop wearing socks, are you? Or draw black lines around your eyes and rub perfume on yourself from samples in magazines and start going all gaga for boys?"

"NO! Of course not!" I told her.

"Good. Because I can only handle one weird sister at a time."

The state of Minnesota had floated away and the capital *H* looked like a number 4 now. The rest of the sky was filled with flying saucer clouds.

"Did you know if you see a fish in the clouds, it's supposed to mean that you're going to be rich?"

"I see a fish!"

"You do not."

"Did you know if you see a frog on skis it's good luck?"

"You just made that up. You have frogs on the brain, Duck."

"Speaking of frogs . . ."

"Yes, Sir Croaks-a-Lot can stay in our room. As long as he doesn't croak-a-lot a lot!"

Cloud Gazing
by Joey Reel

Stevie taught me this cool thing today. Cloud fortune-telling! You can tell fortunes by what shape of cloud you see in the sky. If you see a dinosaur or a fire-breathing dragon or a pig, it means something special.

- Fish = You are super rich; coming into money. (Does a one-fin fish count?)
- Hippo = Oops! Better save your money. You are not super rich. Duh! I knew that when I didn't see a fish! ~S
- Snake = Uh-oh. Trouble. No worries. If you see one, just pretend you don't! A.
- Mountains = Success.
- Ship = Going on a trip. A.k.a. get seasick! ~S
- Hand = You are about to make a new friend. (Lucky Stevie.)
- Kite = You'll go far in life.
- Feather = Believe in yourself. (I saw a turkey. Does that count?) A turkey has feathers. ~S
- Frog on skis = Good luck. You SO made that one up! ~S

I'm going to believe in myself and say YES! —J

Okay, so I made that last one up. But it did bring me good luck because Mom and Dad said I could keep Sir Croaks-a-Lot (not exactly, but they did say, "We'll see how it goes"). ☺

Ten Most Wanted

Cloud homework is cool! I can't wait till sixth grade. I'm helping Stevie make WANTED posters for each type of cloud.

ALTOCUMULUS
Gray patches with sharp edges.
Look in the middle atmosphere
for this one.

STRATUS
This one likes to lay low,
just above the ground.
Looks like wispy fog.

CUMULUS
Known for eating cotton candy!
Big and fluffy.
Harmless as a kitten.

NIMBOSTRATUS
Don't let the name fool you.
This dark character blocks the sun.

CUMULONIMBUS
a.k.a. Cauliflower Face.
Could turn into thunderstorm.

CIRROCUMULUS
Mr. Fish Scales.
Called "mackerel sky."
You'll find him when wind
changes direction.

I Know What You Did (At Camp) Last Summer

I walked Joey home, then grabbed my bike and headed over to Olivia's. She lives in Pleasant Hill Palisades. Dad calls it Potato Skin Palaces. Say no more. Every house is taupe, tan, raw umber, burnt sienna. A.k.a. *brown.*

Inside the front door, I kicked my shoes off and padded upstairs in my sock feet to her room.

"Ta-da!" she said, spinning around her room like a jewelry-box ballerina.

"Ta-da what?" Same four-poster bed with canopy. Same comforter with seven hundred matching pillows. Same everything.

"Duh! I painted my room!"

"Wasn't it always white?"

"It *was* white. Now it's Divine Vanilla. Don't you love it?"

"Yeah, so much I want to lick it," I teased.

We plopped on the floor, talking about everything from homework to her weirdo cello teacher to favorite pizza toppings. While we chatted, I doodled in my science notebook with my cupcake-scented pen.

Then, out of the blue, she hit me with it.

"That kid so likes you."

My pen stopped. "Huh? What kid?"

"You know what kid. The kid sitting behind us at the assembly today. Oscar the Grouch. He is so into you."

"Oh, the kid who got us into detention! He is *not* so into me. You're cracked. G-Y-H-E—Get Your Head Examined."

"Are you kidding? He was only bumping into you on purpose and pulling your hair every other second."

"Yeah. Which only proves how annoying he is. Besides, if he's so into me, then why was he talking to you the whole time?"

"Because. Are you really going to tell me you don't get it? That's what boys do when they like you. They talk to the person that doesn't make them nervous, even though it's the other person they really want to talk to."

"You're wack," I told her. "He just saw me in Earth Science class probably. And he's new. He doesn't know anybody. That's all. Trust me."

Olivia made an exasperated *pfff* sound, ruffling her bangs.

"Do we have to talk about this?" I asked. "You know I hate—Never mind."

"You're still mad at me, aren't you? *Uh!* You are. You're mad. This is about camp last summer, isn't it?"

"What about camp last summer?" I asked in a fakey voice, pretending innocence.

"You know perfectly well what."

"You know what? Sometimes I wish you'd never gone to that stupid camp," I blurted.

"Ha! I knew it!" She lowered her voice and whispered conspiratorially. "Because I held hands with that kid, right?"

"Yeah, some kid you knew for, like, half a second!"

"No way. I knew him."

"What's his name?"

"Matt."

"Matt what?"

"Matt . . . something."

I had doodled Oscar the Grouch, and now I vehemently colored in his garbage can. I don't know why I was cheesed off that my best friend since kindergarten kept talking about boys more and more these days. Maybe I felt left out. Like she was part of a club I didn't belong to. But I didn't even want to be in a club that had to do with boys. I guess I was worried that we'd grow apart.

"Stevie, when are you going to wake up and smell the cookies? Everybody in our grade is getting into stuff."

"What stuff? Going to summer camp?"

"Ha, ha. Very funny. Boy stuff. I know at least two girls our age at school who have boyfriends. And everybody knows Madison Meyers kissed Nick Stephanopoulos . . . in the girls' bathroom!"

"How do you know that wasn't just a big rumor?"

"Trust me. I know. Because Madison told Sierra and Sierra told Sara and Sara told me that he stepped on her toe and crushed it with his big old boy feet."

I let out a snigger.

"There's even a blog about it."

"A blog!"

"Face it. You're going to have to like a boy sometime. Hold hands. Maybe even go out."

"Like on a date? Are you bonkers?" Inside I was secretly wondering, *Why don't I care about this stuff like other girls my age? Was I missing out on something? Am I weird? Is something wrong with me?*

I hated that I was second-guessing myself.

"Are you listening?" Olivia asked, waving a hand at me. "Trust me. You don't want to be a major boy repeller. You might as well just hang garlic around your neck."

"At least I'll keep away vampires."

"Ha, ha," said Olivia, inspecting a patch of paint on the wall.

"I think the paint fumes have gone to your head. For your information, I'm *not* going out with some random kid. It's so completely and totally embarrassing. I mean, parents would have to drive us! And what if he tried to hold hands or something? People would see."

"Okay. I get it. All I'm saying is . . . you should talk to that kid. If you don't know what to talk about, just tell him you need help with your cloud identification project."

"But I don't need help."

"I know you don't need help. But he doesn't know you don't need help. Anyway, it doesn't matter if you need help or not. The point is, you pretend you need help."

"*You* need help," I said. I couldn't help laughing a little.

"Just talk to him. Be a friend. You said yourself he needs a friend."

"Hello! What have I been saying? He's a *boy*! In case you hadn't noticed, I have all sisters. No brothers. I don't know the first thing when it comes to boys."

"What's to know?" Olivia starts ticking stuff off on her fingers. "They like sports and UFOs and pulling wings off bugs and taking stuff apart."

"And you left out the part about how boys can be pretty annoying."

"At first he was kind of annoying, but then he was pretty funny, don't you think?"

Silence. I concentrated on my doodling. I drew a sky full of stars and swirly clouds to rival Van Gogh's. Doodling gave me a chance to half think my own thoughts while Olivia talked her head off, rehashing the conversation from the assembly.

" . . . and you're all, 'My friends call me Stevie,' and laughing and batting your eyelashes," she teased.

I looked up. "I was not batting my eyelashes. A person has to blink!" I protested.

"Whatever . . ."

When I looked back down at my night sky, I'd drawn squiggles, peace signs, a butterfly, a moth, and an owl. The owl had two round Os for eyes, and, without thinking, I'd made them into a pair of glasses.

I closed my notebook with a snap. "I better go. Dad's making his famous curry, and he'll freak if I'm late for dinner."

B Is for Bad Word

The next day, I was tiptoeing into Alex's room, trying not to make noise, when Joey popped up from behind the bed. "AAAGH!" I screeched. "Jo-ey! Stop scaring me like that. What are you doing in here, anyway?"

"What are *you* doing in here?" she asked.

"I asked you first," I said.

"Okay, okay I didn't want to tell you, but when I got home from school, Sir Croaks-a-Lot was not in his tank. He escaped! I don't know how he got out, and I know I'm not supposed to be in here when Alex isn't home, but I thought I heard him in here and he might be hiding."

"I'll help you look, Duck. Alex will freak if she finds a frog in her room."

I crawled around on hands and knees, helping Joey look for her frog. We looked under the bed, behind the desk, even under the rug. "How come frogs never croak when you're looking for them?" I asked.

"I don't know," said Joey. "Maybe if we stop looking, he'll start croaking."

"Here froggy, froggy," I called.

"So, what were you coming in here for?" Joey asked.

"None of your beeswax. I was looking for my . . . poetry book I'm using for Language Arts, if you must know."

"It's on your bed in our room."

"Oh, I guess it was my Earth Science book—"

"In your backpack. Also on the bed."

"Whatever, Miss Snoopy Pants." The truth is, I didn't want to admit to Joey I was looking for one of Alex's magazines or a book—anything that might help me with The Truth About Boys.

I stood up and ran my finger across the spines of books on Alex's shelf. *Speak. Cut. Crush. Glass. Sold. Feed. Fade. Flipped. Prom. Prep. Peeled. Sleep. Wake.*

Beige. Lost. Gone. Sheesh! No wonder teenagers grunt and speak in one-syllable words.

Twisted. Trouble. Loser. Lucky. I Was a Teenage Fairy. What do you know? Seven whole syllables.

"I don't think a frog would be hiding inside a book," said Joey. "Unless he's an origami frog."

I returned *Lucky* to the shelf and straightened the spines of the books, lining them back up the way they were.

Joey peered into Alex's closet. "Hey, I know. Maybe Sir Croaks-a-Lot is hiding with Alex's journal, you know, in the shoebox in the closet under the fleece blanket she made in Girl Scouts one time."

"So, he's not hiding in a book, but he can read Alex's journal?"

Joey shrugged. "I'm just saying."

"Did you try her dresser?" I asked.

"Are you kidding? She'll kill me if I go in there."

"Well, she'll kill you worse for going in her closet and reading her journal. Besides, how do we know he's even in here?"

"C'mon, Stevie. Help! What if Alex comes home any second and catches us?"

“Us?”

“Please?”

“Shh. Quiet,” I whispered, holding my finger up to my lips. *Creck-eck. Creck-eck.*

Joey’s eyes got as round as marbles. The sound was coming from the direction of the dresser. I pointed and motioned for Joey to check it out.

Joey and I started opening drawers and rummaging through stuff. The top drawer was just one big tangle of junk—from heart-shaped rocks to headbands to Hello Kitty key chains.

Joey pawed through Alex’s underwear drawer.

“Joey, not in there!”

“How do you know?”

“Hey, look at this!” Joey held up a pair of light blue undies. “They have writing on them. What’s *Vendredi* mean?”

“How should I know? Sounds like some kind of sports car to me.” Joey and I peered more closely at the words—*Mercredi, Jeudi, Vendredi* . . .

“It’s the days of the week in French!” I proclaimed, too loudly.

“But Alex takes Spanish,” said Joey. I shrugged my shoulders.

"Keep looking."

"Maybe he's in here," said Joey. "Maybe he's hiding in Alex's T-shirts because they're all soft and cozy."

Joey flipped through a stack of folded tank tops and T-shirts. "Hey, all these shirts have words."

TROUBLEMAKER. VERY IMPORTANT PRINCESS. RARE BIRD. FREAK OF NATURE.

"Geez," I said to Joey. "Who knew Alex had so many tanks, huh?"

"Every single one has writing. She could wear them all at one time and be a walking encyclopedia."

I couldn't help cracking up as I looked through a drawer full of jeans.

Joey was still in the T-shirt drawer, and she kept reading them off. BRAT. HIP CHICK. OREGON. PEACE. ACT UP. "Where'd she get all these, anyway? I've never seen her wear half of them. Why is she hiding them?"

"She probably layers and wears them under stuff. And she doesn't want us to know because then we'll want to wear them too.

"Not me," said Joey. "Well, maybe the PEACE shirt."

She dug down to the bottom of the pile. "BAD APPLE, BAD TO THE BONE, B—" Suddenly Joey screeched *"Ahhh!"* and let the shirt go like it was hot.

"What? What's wrong?"

"I almost said a swear!" Joey slapped her hand to her mouth, covering it as if trying to push the word back in.

"What? What do you mean?"

"Mom gets really mad if we swear and we're not even supposed to swear in Shakespeare too much, you know, like how Alex calls us milk-livered maggot-pies and stuff." Joey stabbed her finger at the bottom drawer. "In there. See for yourself. At the bottom of the pile." She spat out the words. "Alex has a shirt with the *B* word on it!"

"She does not."

"Wanna bet? A hundred dollars."

I was sure Joey was wrong. I was sure that the shirt probably just said *Witch.* But when I yanked the shirt out from the bottom of the pile, there it was: the *B* word, emblazoned across the shirt in fancy cursive!

"See? What did I tell you? Give it. I'm telling Mom!"

My heart was pounding, like I'd discovered some deep, dark secret of Alex's that I wasn't supposed to know. I don't know why, but I didn't hand over the shirt to Joey. I hurriedly stuffed it way down deep in the bottom of the drawer.

"C'mon, Joey," I said, yanking her by the arm. "Let's get out of here. Now. Before Alex finds out." My voice sounded wobbly. "We shouldn't be snooping." I stared at my trembling hand. I felt far away, like I didn't know my own hand anymore.

Really, it was my sister I didn't know anymore. Alex. Who was the Alex who would wear that shirt?

"But what about Sir Croaks-a-Lot? You said Alex would freak if—"

"Never mind what I said," I told my little sister. For some reason, I couldn't stay there another minute. I had to get away from that shirt.

Once Upon a Frog
by Joey Reel

If Alex can talk to a sock monkey,
I can talk to a frog.

Hey, little guy, you scared me. Yes, you did. I thought you were lost. How did you get out of your tank? I wish you could talk.

Don't ever grow up or become an ugly old toad or turn into a prince, okay? You and me have to stick together. Yes, we do.

Creck-eck. Creck-eck.

What? You want me to tell you a story? Here goes:

Once upon a time . . . there was a brave knight named Sir Lancelot. Hey! What am I saying? I mean a brave frog named Sir Croaks-a-Lot. One day, he hopped far outside his kingdom in search of the Holy Snail and ended up far, far away (down the hall) in the Land of Bad Words. It was dark. It was scary. It smelled like a teenager. Then, along came a damsel not in distress (Yours Truly) and rescued him from an evil pit full of vipers (a.k.a. Alex's trash can full of used tissues). And he lived happily ever after because he never ran away again.

SECOND MUSHROOM FROM THE LEFT
Starring Alex

Me: Sock Monkey, O Sock Monkey. Wherefore art thou, Sock Monkey?

Sock Monkey: I'm right here. So? How'd the audition go? Are you Juliet?

Me: Don't ask. I so totally blew it.

Sock Monkey: I thought you weren't going to know till tomorrow.

Me: Trust me. I know.

Sock Monkey: Is this like one of those times when you *pretend* you blew it but really you aced it? I don't want to hear it. I'd cover my ears, if I had any.

Me: Thou art a villain.

Sock Monkey: A villain made of socks? I hardly think so.

Me: Okay, I know when it comes to auditions, I always say I blew it, but what if I told you this time, it's really, truly, actually true? Sorry to have to break it to you, my friend, but they will be writing about this one in "sour misfortune's book."

Sock Monkey: But you've wanted this your whole life. You know Juliet's lines backward and forward. How could anybody else get the part? You don't even have to read from the script for the balcony scene, and *nobody* has died more times than you. Besides, you look great dead.

Me: See, everybody knows when you try out for Juliet, you can't just get up there and *do* Juliet. Because the director has seen the same thing a thousand times.

Sock Monkey: Really? That's weird to try out for Juliet and not be Juliet.

Me: That's just it. You do something else to show them you can do Juliet.

Sock Monkey: So, what'd you do?

Me: Promise you won't tell anybody? Especially Stevie. And Joey.

Sock Monkey: *(Holds up a sock paw.)* Sock Monkey's honor.

Me: *(Hangs head.)* I sang.

Sock Monkey: You what? You sang? As in a song? That's Stevie's thing. You know you're horrible at singing. Why would you do that?

Me: I didn't mean to! See, I rewrote this one Juliet scene, you know, in my own words. To make sure I really had the meaning down. So I actually did that for my monologue, thinking it would be super unique.

Sock Monkey: That sounds kind of cool.

Me: Yeah, except it wasn't. And Mr. Cannon kept crinkling his eyebrows. Then I said the words "innocent as a rose," and it made me think of that song from *Sound of Music*, so I just started singing "Sixteen Going on Seventeen."

Sock Monkey: *(Silence.)*

Me: Say something.

Sock Monkey: What did Mr. Cannon do?

Me: Nothing. He just sat in his chair. He didn't clap. He didn't say "Good job" or "Nice effort" or "Bravo" or anything.

Sock Monkey: Well, maybe it was like a poker face—he doesn't want to give it away. You know, who he's picking for Juliet.

Me: The worst part is, he didn't scribble any notes. He always scribbles notes on his yellow tablet. Instead, he just thanked me and looked down at his clipboard.

Sock Monkey: Maybe you were actually good and he didn't need to make notes.

Me: But there were tons of other girls flinging their hair around and saying, "Romeo, Romeo," and he made notes on them.

Sock Monkey: But think about it. He knows your work. You have way more experience. You've been in tons of plays, like *Beauty and the Beast.*

Me: That's just it. What if he wants somebody new? Somebody different? What if he's thinking that I already had a shot at the lead when I got to be Beauty and Scott was Beast. Oh, no. What if he doesn't want us to be together again? Or what if he decides to give somebody else a chance?

Sock Monkey: Somebody like maybe . . . Jayden Pffeffer?

Me: Uh! Don't even say that name. It makes my blood boil. Queen Aggravating.

Sock Monkey: What does Queen Aggravating have that you haven't got?

Me: Long hair, for one thing. She looks exactly like Juliet.

Sock Monkey: But Mr. Cannon isn't going to pass you over just because you have short hair. He knows there's more to acting than looking the part, right?

Me: Her audition *was* pretty lame.

Sock Monkey: What did she do?

Me: A Princess Mia monologue from *The Princess Diaries*. It wasn't great, but it was better than mine! *What* was I thinking?

Sock Monkey: C'mon. You're always freaked out about Jayden. And most of the time you end up with the lead, and she has to be your understudy.

Me: Not always. Once she got to be the bunny in *Mushroom in the Rain*, and I had to be, like, Second Mushroom from the Left.

Sock Monkey: In kindergarten!

Me: But Mr. Cannon scribbled down tons of notes after Jayden's audition. He even had to flip over a page on his tablet.

Sock Monkey: Ooh, this *is* bad.

Me: It is! Now Princess Mia is going to get the part and Jayden Pffeffer is going to kiss Romeo. *My* Romeo. In front of the whole entire world. And he's going to be a prince, not a toad, and kiss her back. Owww!

Sock Monkey: You don't know that.

Me: Just tell me it's going to be okay.

Sock Monkey: It's going to be okay . . . hey, stop shaking meeeeee!

Got Frog?
by Joey Reel

I would never, never, ever, never
Kiss a boy, even if his name was Scott Frog.

Ten reasons why frogs are better than boys:

1. FROGS are from the Kingdom Animalia.
   BOYS are from Planet Alien.
2. FROGS have bumps. BOYS have scabs!
3. FROGS eat insects, which helps the ecosystem.
   BOYS eat French fries that fall on the floor, which helps the custodian but is disgusting.
4. FROGS aren't slimy. BOYS are sweaty.
5. FROGS have webbed feet.
   BOYS have stinky feet. Fact!
6. FROGS stick out their tongues for a reason.
   BOYS stick out their tongues — at girls — for no reason.

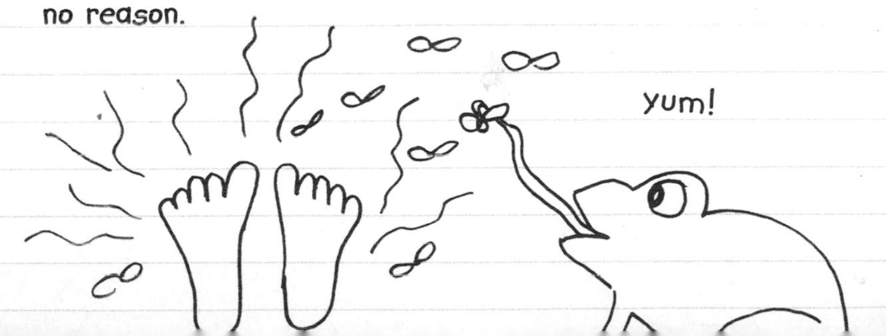

7. FROGS are loud because they're singing.
   BOYS are loud all the time, even during Silent Sustained Reading.
8. FROGS don't throw paper airplanes.
   BOYS throw them at your head.
9. FROGS are friendly.
   BOYS call you by your last name.
10. FROGS (like Sir Croaks-a-Lot) are just plain cute.
   BOYS are just plain weird!

See Alex.
Alex Is Sick.
Oh, Alex!

On Thursday morning, Alex would not open the door to her room. What was she doing in there? Probably trying on that *blankety-blank* shirt that she didn't want anyone to see. Ever since finding it yesterday, a feeling had started in the pit of my stomach. Kind of like when you're a kid on roller skates going down a hill and are not sure if you can stop.

"Hurry up, Alex. I made French toast," I said, trying to sound normal. "We're going to miss the bus and Dad'll be mad if he has to drive us. Again."

Mom opened the door to Alex's room, pressing a button on the thermometer. "Honey, Alex isn't feeling well." She felt Alex's forehead. Alex was still in her

Dick and Jane pajamas, propped up against a mountain of pillows, trying to look pathetic. Plus, she had some serious bed head going on. Not pretty.

"You're not even dressed?" I asked. My voice sounded edgy inside my own head, and I couldn't keep my eyes from looking at the drawer with the T-shirt. *Why was that stupid shirt bugging me so much?*

"I'm sick," she croaked, clutching her throat. "Can't you tell?"

"But you're going to school, right?"

"I told Alex she doesn't have to go today," said Mom. "Here. See if you're running a fever. Leave this in for three minutes. Are you sure you'll be okay?"

Alex nodded. Outside, the sky was darkening. Heavy gray clouds threatened more rain. Mom flicked on Alex's bedside lamp, a small circle of warmth against the gloom.

"I'm late for work, but I'll make sure Dad comes up to check on you in a bit." Mom headed downstairs.

Alex yanked the thermometer out of her mouth.

"You are so not sick," I said. "I can't believe Mom actually believed you."

"Why wouldn't she?"

"Oh, I don't know, maybe because you don't have a fever or a sore throat and you're not covered in measles or chicken pox. So unless you have the Queen Mab plague . . ."

My sister clutched her stomach. "I think I have food poisoning from the dinner you made last night."

"All I made was the mashed potatoes. Dad made the rest. Besides, you don't get food poisoning from mashed potatoes."

"You do if they taste like cotton balls!"

Sheesh. Can I help it if Joey stored a bunch of cotton balls in an empty marshmallow bag and Mom accidentally put them away in the kitchen cupboard and they fell out and landed in the potatoes? "I fished them out," I told her. I'd sooner have believed a frog in her throat.

"Okay. So I don't have food poisoning. But I think I might have skittles."

"Skittles?" I asked. "Isn't that a candy? Unless you have fruit-flavored chicken pox. Never mind. I don't even want to know."

Alex slunk down and pulled the covers up to her chin. I could still see a curly-headed kid with overalls and a red balloon and the words *Jump, Puff. Jump, jump, jump. Oh, Puff* on the piece of pajamas sticking out from under the covers. I couldn't help letting out a laugh.

"It's not funny."

"You can't be sick. Not today. Isn't today the day you find out if you got the part of Juliet?"

Alex started fake-coughing.

I opened my eyes wide and pointed at my sister. "Wait a second. Now I get it. You don't want to go to school because . . . you don't want to find out the Drama Club results because . . . you're afraid you didn't get the part! Ha!"

"Whatever, Sherlock. You've got a whole little mystery going on there, but it has nothing to do with reality. I told you, I'm sick." She hunkered down under the covers some more, trying to look miserable.

"You're not *that* good an actress," I said.

"Join the club."

"What club?"

"The club of people who don't think I'm a good actress."

This is the part where I'm supposed to tell my

sister how great she is at acting, reassure her, make her feel better. Like I always did. But I wasn't sure anymore—was this the same Alex I knew yesterday?

She looked like the same Alex she'd always been, minus the long hair, of course. On one hand, she wore Dick and Jane pajamas and talked to her sock monkey. On the other hand, she read one-syllable titled books about things I didn't understand, harbored smuggled T-shirts in her bottom drawer, and secretly wanted to kiss a boy.

This was definitely *not* turning out to be a French toast kind of morning. I could almost feel the atmospheric pressure in the room. I rubbed my temples. It made my head ache, trying to figure this stuff out. Besides, I had problems of my own. Like in-class detention after school today.

"Hey, can I ask you a question? Have you ever had in-class detention?"

"Sure. Lots of times. Why do you ask?"

"No reason."

"Wait! *You* got detention?" Alex must have seen my face fall, because she said, "It's no biggie. It's not like detention with a capital *D* where you have to go to the library and spend two hours with a bunch of delinquents."

"Ha, ha. Very funny."

"Look, you just stay after and help your homeroom teacher. Once I had to write a short essay about some famous genius that flunked out of middle school. But most times there's nothing for you to do, so you get to play Sudoku."

How did Alex know so much about big- or little-*D* detention? First the shirt, now this . . . Or maybe she *got* detention for wearing that shirt to school?

"So, are you coming to school or not?"

"Not."

"Well, don't think I'm going to go look at the Drama Club list and find out for you. I can't, anyway."

"Can't? Or won't?" Silence. Alex flipped over onto her side, facing away from me. "Fine."

"Fine," I said, turning to go.

"Can you at least get my homework?" Alex asked. "Algebra and biology."

"Boy-ology," I muttered. It just came out. In less than thirty minutes, I'd gone from making French toast for my sister to acting as mean as stinging sleet.

"And bring me home some Skittles?"

"You are *so* not funny."

Just then, the sky opened up and rain slashed the window.

Great. Now I'd get poured on. I'd really have to run if I hoped to have a prayer of catching the bus. One more late slip might land me in *bad kids* detention. In capital-*D* detention, I would *not* be playing Sudoku.

A Bad Case of Boyitis

The day just went from bad to worse.

I was sitting in Earth Science, my favorite class at the moment, when out of nowhere, a wadded-up note hit me in the head. I looked around. Olivia wasn't even in this class.

I opened it a teeny-tiny bit to try to read it without someone, a.k.a. Wire Rims, spying on me. *Not coming to detention after school. Sorry!* It was signed with a fancy letter *O,* big enough to rival Oprah's autograph. Like that was supposed to make it not so bad.

Olivia. How did she do that? She must have given it to somebody else to pass to me. I was thinking how

I'd never speak to her again if she left me alone with Wire Rims, when an announcement crackled over the loudspeaker.

"Stevie Reel to the front office. Mr. Petry? Is Stevie Reel in class? Please send him down to the office."

Him? The whole class erupted in laughter. Suddenly Mr. Petry's giant jellyfish weather phenomenon was not so interesting. All eyes were on me. I felt my face go thermal and turn bright red. Weather alert: global warming had just reached classroom 11.

"Did they say *Steven* Reel?" somebody asked.

"Hey, Reel, make sure you don't stop in the *boys'* bathroom on the way to the office," somebody else jeered.

I zoomed out of there before I had to hear the standard string of sixth-grade-boys-being-jerks jokes.

The office! Now what? Did I do something wrong? I hope I didn't have capital-*D* detention. But Dad had already signed off on the paper saying I had to stay after school. Did something happen? Somebody got hurt? Alex was sick for real and they rushed her to the emergency room?

I hurried over to the woman at the main desk who

was clicking her yellow happy-face nails a mile a minute on the keyboard. "Hi, um, I'm Stevie Reel."

"You're Stevie?" she asked, glancing up but still clicking. "I was expecting—never mind. Your mom's on the phone."

"My mom?" I asked, like I hadn't heard from her in a hundred years or something. *Why isn't Mom at the studio?*

"You can take it on that phone." She nodded to a desk in the corner. "Just press line three."

"Mom?" I asked. "Is everything okay? Why are you calling me in the middle of—"

"It's me, okay?" the voice said. "I had to talk to you."

"Alex?" I whispered. "W-what are you . . . where are you . . . why are you . . ." I stammered. Finally, I eked out a whole sentence. "I was in the middle of a class, *Mom,*" I said for the benefit of Happy Nails. "Why are you calling me?"

"Sorry I got you out of class, but—"

"You told them you were Mom? You scared me half to death! I thought it was some kind of emergency!"

"It *is* an emergency. I'm going crazy. I can't take it anymore. I have to know."

"Know what?" I asked, looking around guiltily.

"You know. About the play. Who got the part of Juliet? You have to look at the list for me."

"I'm not—I can't—" Still sputtering.

"What's the big deal? Just go over to the auditorium and check the Drama Club list. It'll be posted on the bulletin board outside Mr. Cannon's door as soon as school's over. You know, the same as it was for *Once Upon a Mattress.*"

"I can't believe you. You fake sick and don't come to school because you think you didn't get the part and now you want *me* to find out for you? I've got problems of my own, you know. I can't. Even if I wanted to, I have to stay after. For detention. *Comprende?*" Just then, Happy Nails walked past with a stack of papers.

"Stevie, just run down there as soon as the bell rings, please? It'll take two seconds."

"Sorry, *Mom.* I didn't mean to worry you. I know I forgot my lunch, but Olivia gave me half of hers. And, no, I don't need my violin. Orchestra is on Thursdays."

"Stevie . . ." Alex urged.

"Okay. Love you too. I'll see you at home. *Bye, Mom!*"

I walked back to class, fuming about Alex. But before I reached room 11, the bell rang and everybody poured into the hall. I rushed over to Olivia, who was spacing out in front of her open locker.

"What do you mean you're not going to be at detention?" I practically screamed. "How can you skip detention? It's detention! They'll give you another detention for missing detention."

"Stevie, I think you just got the Guinness world record for saying 'detention.'" Olivia glanced around to see if anybody was staring at us.

Right-left-right. I spun the dial on my lock, yanking open my own locker so hard the door vibrated angrily. "You had all day to tell me this. You couldn't have told me on the bus or at lunch or this morning in Language Arts?"

"I'm telling you now. I have an orthodontist appointment and I had to wait months to get it. And I'm not about to miss my one chance to get the last of these braces off." She flashed the shiny silver on her four front teeth at me. "No way am I waiting one more day. One more minute. Look out, popcorn, here I come!"

"And Ms. Carter-Dunne said that was okay?"

"I told her I had a dental emergency. She said I could make it up Friday."

"Sheesh. Faking sick sure is going around. Maybe I can catch it too."

"Huh?"

"Nothing." I turned to my friend and pleaded. "Liv, please. I'm your best friend. *Please* don't leave me alone with him."

"Who him?"

"You know who him." I lowered my voice. "Wire Rims."

"Oh. Him. So that's what you're all bent out of shape about?"

"Hello!" I said in a voice that came out high and shrieky. "I told you, I don't know the first thing about boys." She knew when it came to boys I hadn't the foggiest. But she pretended like it wasn't a big deal.

"So?" She shrugged. "I already told you. They have big clown feet, they grunt instead of talking, they're always hungry, and they like to burp."

"Be serious," I told my friend.

"I *am* being serious. See?" She sucked in her cheeks to keep from smiling. Her eyes popped out at me.

"Okay, now you just look like a demented circus clown. C'mon, Livvie. I don't know what to say to the guy. You know I'm bad at this stuff." Not like Olivia. When it came to trying new things, she did not hesitate to dive right in. Brave. Fearless.

"It's detention. You don't have to talk. You can flirt with your eyes." She blinked her eyes, fluttering her eyelashes madly.

"Okay, now you look like a demented circus clown with something stuck in her eye."

"Look, trust me, there's nothing to stress about. First of all, you're not supposed to talk in detention anyway, right? So, you don't have to talk to him."

"I can't just not talk to him. Then he'll think I hate him."

"Guys aren't like girls. They don't read a bunch of stuff into talking, or not talking. When it comes to boys, it is what it is. Simple."

"There's nothing simple about it."

Olivia stepped back, studying me up and down.

"What?"

"Nothing. Just . . . why do you care so much?" Olivia gave me a hard look. "Time out! You like him. You are so crushing on the Glasses Man!" she teased.

"Shh! I'm not crushing on anybody!" I said, keeping my teeth clenched. I glanced around to make sure nobody heard us.

"You'll be fine. I promise. Just remember, if he cracks his knuckles, that means he wants to hold hands. And if he takes his glasses off, that means he likes you."

"Wait. What?"

"Kidding! But not about the first thing."

I couldn't tell if she was making fun of me or not.

"Besides, it's better this way. Without me there, he'll have to talk to you. Instead of talking through me to talk to you."

Dear Ms. Carter-Dunne,
Unfortunately, Stevie Reel had to go home sick and won't be able to make detention after school today. I'm afraid she has a bad case of Boyitis.

I wish.

What is YOUR lucky number?

It's all in a name. YOUR name.
Use your name to
find out your fortune.

1. Write out your first and last name.

2. Find the matching number for each letter of your name.

A	B	C	D	E	F	G	H	I		J	K	L	M	N	O	P	Q	R		S	T	U	V	W	X	Y	Z
1	2	2	4	5	8	3	8	1		1	2	3	4	5	7	8	1	2		3	4	6	6	6	6	1	7

3. Add up all the numbers.

S O C K M O N K E Y
3 + 7 + 2 + 2 4 + 7 + 5 + 2 + 5 + 1 = 38

4. You will end up with a 2-digit number (38). Now add the first number to the second number. Keep adding until you have ONE number.

3 + 8 = 11, 1 + 1 = 2

5. What does your lucky number say about you? Consult the Lucky Number Chart on the next page.

1 You are confident, outgoing, a natural leader (even if you are bossy sometimes), and a pioneer!

2 You are caring and sensitive and enjoy helping others. You are good at making peace.

3 You are a creative, positive person, happy with life. For you, the eternal optimist, the glass is always half full.

4 You are reliable and dependable, practical and down-to-earth, a good and faithful friend.

5 You have a good sense of humor and a witty and curious mind. You get along well with others.

6 You are giving and caring and will do well in business and handling money. Lots of money! You'll go far with your ideals.

7 You are relaxed, calm and quiet, and a great thinker who dreams of a better world.

8 You are generous and trustworthy. A good organizer, you can handle responsibility and will persevere.

9 You are charming, compassionate, and have an appealing personality. You seek to understand yourself and others.

Detention

2:55

De·ten·tion (noun) [di-'ten-chən]

1. confinement, imprisonment *with a boy*
2. punishment by being detained after school *with a boy*
3. locked up, incarcerated *with a boy*

Okay, so I added the *"with a boy"* part. But still!

3:01

So far, no Sudoku in sight. Maybe the real punishment is just to worry about what our punishment will be.

Outside, the rain had stopped. But fog had swallowed up the mountains and settled over the parking lot, turning the playground into a scene from *Macbeth.*

I sat at my regular homeroom desk. Wire Rims slid into the seat next to me.

"Hey, Stevie."

"Hey . . . Wire Rims."

"So, you like the glasses, huh? I get that a lot. Comments on the glasses, I mean." He took off his glasses and rubbed them with the hem of his shirt. He smiled a crooked, goofy smile.

Ms. Carter-Dunne told us we could sit quietly and work on our Language Arts homework for class—a five-paragraph persuasive essay. Mine argued against hunting wolves in Oregon. But I found it hard to concentrate on wolves when I could feel Wire Rims looking at me.

Why hadn't I used my peppermint body wash this morning? Now I just smell like dumb old soap.

Why did he have to sit so close?

Why were my ears turning red for no reason?

Why was he cracking his knuckles?

Why was my heart beating in my throat?

Why was he not pretending to do his homework?

Why was he looking over at my essay? What was his essay about?

Why did I even care about any of this?

Forget detention. This felt like a class in Lameology 101.

Stare straight ahead, I willed myself. *Stop stealing glances at him.*

Forget wolves. I took out my Science notebook and tried to concentrate on homework. But instead of observing clouds, I observed the specimen sitting next to me.

OBSERVATION: *Shaggy blond hair*
CONCLUSIONS:
Surfer dude?
Skateboard dude?
Band-member wannabe?
Yeti tendencies?

OBSERVATION: *Wire-rimmed glasses*
CONCLUSIONS:
Geek potential? Nouveau geek?
Wants to look smart?
Techie?
Trying to hide eyes?

Can't afford contacts?
Entering John Lennon look-alike contest?
Has ommetaphobia: fear of eyeballs?

OBSERVATION: *Faded T-shirt:* THAI ONE ON
CONCLUSIONS:
Likes chicken on a stick?
Family owns Thai restaurant?
Older brother hand-me-down?
Likes puns; wordplay freak?

OBSERVATION: *Absence of burping*
CONCLUSIONS:
Hasn't eaten since early lunch?
Trying to be polite around a girl?
Has burpophobia?

3:17

All of a sudden, Wire Rims reached over and tapped me. "Ah!" I nearly jumped out of my skin. Ms. Carter-Dunne glanced up. When she looked down at her papers again, Wire Rims pointed to the door.

Scott Towel! What in the world? He was hovering

just outside the doorway, gesturing like a crazy person. I glanced over at Wire Rims. He shrugged. Scott was mouthing words and motioning for me to come out into the hallway. I couldn't tell what he was saying, but his eyes were about to pop out of his head, which looked positively volcanic. I figured I better get out there before his head exploded or something.

"Excuse me," I said, clearing my throat. "Ms. Carter-Dunne? Can I go to my locker and get a book I need?"

"No problem," she said, glancing up at me.

I hurried out into the hall. A hand grabbed my elbow and dragged me into the empty classroom next door.

"Where's Alex?"

"At home." His T-shirt said WILL POWER and had a picture of William Shakespeare's head.

"What do you mean 'at home'? There's a Drama Club meeting today. Right now. They just posted all the parts for *Romeo and Juliet.*"

"She's still at home."

"Is she sick? Oh, man. This is *so* not good. You're not gonna believe this. C'mere. I have to show you something."

"Are you insane?"

"C'mon. Five minutes. You gotta come with me. You're not gonna believe it," he said again.

"I'm in detention!" I told him. "Ms. Carter-Dunne thinks I just went to my locker. I'm already in enough trouble. Do you want me to get another detention for ditching detention?" I glanced toward the door.

"What'd you do?"

"Nothing. I mean—I gotta get back."

"Wait. Look. Here's the thing. The thing is—"

"Hurry up! What's the thing?"

"I think Mr. Cannon went loco or something. I don't know what's eating him. I got the part of Romeo and all, but not a lot of guys even tried out. But the thing is . . . the thing is that . . . Alex didn't get the lead! Okay, so her audition didn't go so great, but she's obviously the best, and he knows it."

Alex didn't get the part! I tried to take in what Scott was telling me. For all my sister's moaning and groaning, it never occurred to me that there would come a time when she actually wouldn't get the role she wanted in a play. "You mean . . . she's n-not Juliet?" I stuttered.

"This is what I'm saying! Crazy, huh?"

"Who got it?"

"Jayden. Jayden Pffeffer."

"Fluffernutter?" I asked incredulously. "Fluffernutter got the lead?" I tried to picture Jayden Pffeffer as Juliet. "This is going to kill Alex."

So much for Alex's first kiss. It had just become the kiss of death.

De-Tension

3:22

When I got back to the classroom, I said, "Sorry, um, I couldn't find my book. Guess I left it at home."

"Well, tell you what. Why don't you two help me out with a project, hmm?" She took us over to the magnetic poetry board in the shape of a refrigerator door, hanging on the back wall.

"You want us to make up similes and metaphors, like in class?" I asked.

"Not today. The magnets have gotten so much use lately that they're all mixed up." She looked at her watch. "Why don't you two spend the last half hour sorting them out for me?" She handed us boxes for

Shakespeare magnets, Seventies magnets, and Text Message magnets. "Try your best to get them into the right trays. And if you're not sure, just make a separate pile."

We started taking magnets off the board. "I guess all the 'thees' and 'thous' go into the Shakespeare tray, huh?" I said, getting started.

Wire Rims didn't say anything. He was peering at a couple of magnets that said *lily-livered* and *canker-blossom.*

"Here, I'll take all the Shakespeare, and you find all the 'Groovy' and 'Far out' ones from the Seventies. Okay?"

"Sure." Wire Rims pulled *Dream On, Can you dig it?,* and *Phoney Baloney* off the board.

"So," Wire Rims asked. "Who was that guy?"

"What guy? Oh, him? Nobody. His name's Scott Towel. I mean, Scott Howell. He's just some guy who my sister kinda, sorta, um, knows."

"He's in eighth?"

"Yeah."

I handed him *cheesy.* He handed me *dafadilly.*

"So . . ." He reached into his backpack and pulled out

a snack pack of two chocolate cupcakes. "Cupcake?" he offered.

"No, thanks."

"Are you sure? There's supposed to be a delight no matter how small a bite," he said, referring to the corny ad for snack cakes. He tore open the package and took a bite. "Did you know every one of these cupcakes has seven loops on top? It's like a thing." When he smiled, his teeth were covered in chocolate.

"A thing, huh?"

"You like cupcakes, right? I mean, you were in a cooking contest or something?"

"How do you know about that?"

"I heard a rumor." He picked up *funkadelic* and *cheese weasel* and tossed them into the Seventies tray.

"Olivia, right?"

He nodded. "I heard you made an entire castle and it was really cool."

I could feel the edges of my mouth curling up into a smile. "Okay, just so you know, you can't believe everything Olivia says."

He pushed a bunch of words to the bottom of the board, spelling out a message for me to see.

Hey Sunshine. U R stellular. Totally munga.

I arranged some Shakespeare magnets to form a message back to him.

Methinks u jest squire (Me, Stevie)

I M no cheese weasel (Wire Rims)

Aye perchance a merry maggot-pie (Me, Stevie)

Grody! (Wire Rims)

3:55

Ms. Carter-Dunne stood up and straightened the stack of papers she'd been reading, tapping them into a neat pile. She started shoving folders into her shoulder bag. "Okay. Time's up, you two. You're free to go."

Thou from loathsome prison breaks

Check ya later Sweetness

The word *Sweetness* dangled at the end of *Check ya later.* Did he mean me? Does that mean he likes me? I caught myself kind of hoping, but it scared me at the same time. What does it mean, anyway, if a boy likes you? Maybe he hadn't even put it there on purpose. Maybe the word just happened to be there.

Uh! I hate that I'm driving myself crazy over a B-O-Y.

No matter what Olivia says, this figuring-out-boys thing was harder than it looked! Definitely *not* a science.

Next time, maybe I'll just start a burping contest.

A Rose Is a Rose Is a Rose
by Just Joey

Romeo and Juliet has some of the most famous quotes — right up there with "To be or not to be." There's even one about a raven — that's how Mom and Dad got the name the Raven for our theater!

- Parting is such sweet sorrow.
- What light through yonder window breaks.
- O Romeo, Romeo, Wherefore art thou Romeo?
- Whiter than new snow on a raven's back
- A rose by any other name would smell as sweet. (My fave!)

Real and actual names of roses that I did not make up:

- Admired Miranda
- Apothecary's Rose So totally Shakespeare. A.
- Baby Blanket
- Bazarre Triumphote How bizarre! ~S
- Chuckles (I am not making this up.)

MWA!

- Creepy
- First Kiss (Bluck!) My fave! A.
- Fortune Teller Cool! A.
- Gourmet Popcorn I have to go water my Gourmet Popcorn! Ha, ha. ~S
- Hugs 'n' Kisses (Bluck x 2.)
- Just Joey (My fave!!!!!!!!!!!!!!) Duh! A.+S
- Outta the Blue (Huh? It's a rose, not a frog.)
- Pinocchio You're lying, right? ~S
- Robin Hood (I kid you not.)
- Seven Sisters Cool! Why not three sisters? ~S
- Voodoo Ooh! My second fave. A.
- Win-Win

← Robin in a hood

Flowers from Shakespeare's plays:
(We have the deck of cards.)

- Rose (*Romeo and Juliet*)
- Belladonna (*Romeo and Juliet*)
- Monkshood (*Henry IV*)
- Hemlock (*Macbeth*)
- Daisy (*Love's Labours Lost*)
- Pansy (*Hamlet*)
- Daffodil (*The Winter's Tale*)
- Lily (*King John*)
- Cowslip (*The Tempest*)

Birds in *Romeo and Juliet*:

- Lark
- Raven!!!!!!
- Nightingale
- Rooster
- Goose
- Falcon
- Snowy Dove

TO TELL OR NOT TO TELL
Starring Alex

Me: Finally! Stevie. You're home. What took you so long? Did you see the list? Hurry up, hurry up. Tell me. I've been dying all day.

Joey: Yeah, Stevie. Hurry up. Tell her.

Me: No, wait. *(Takes a deep breath to calm down.)* Don't tell me.

Joey: Yeah, Stevie, don't tell her.

Me: Joey, do you have to keep saying everything I say? And do you have to keep bringing that frog in my room?

Joey: He has a name.

Stevie: Tell you or don't tell you? I feel like a Ping-Pong ball. First you drag me out of class and pretend to be Mom because you can't wait to find out; now you don't want me to tell you?

Me: So, you know!

Joey: You have to tell her sometime.

Me: That's bad, right? What did you mean,

Joey, she'll have to tell me sometime? Just tell me. Okay, go ahead. I'm ready. No. Wait. First . . . *(Gets into Shakespeare mode.)* "Is the news good or bad, answer to that."

Stevie: Well, let's see. It depends.

Me: On what?

Stevie: On whether or not you were hoping to have a lot of extra free time.

Me: *(Glares.)* Oh, spurious day! How can this be happening to me? Uh! I knew it! I knew it the second Mr. Cannon didn't take notes. I didn't get the part, did I?

Stevie: *(Cringes.)* No. You're not Juliet.

Me: What sayest thou? Hast thou not a word of joy? Some comfort?

Stevie: I'm sorry, Alex.

Joey: But look at the bright side. *(In baby-talk voice.)* Right, Sir Croaks-a-Lot?

Me: What bright side? You sound like Dad with his "Every cloud has a silver lining" speech. This is only the worst day of my life.

Joey: Um . . . *(Thinks.)* You don't have to pretend to drink poison and die and stab yourself in the stomach. *(Stevie nods in agreement.)* And you don't have to kiss a yucky boy who has Frog Lips in front of tons of people.

Me: *(Falls back on the bed and moans.)* My life is over.

Stevie: Your life is not over. It's *one* part in one play.

Me: The role of a lifetime!

Stevie: There are other parts, Alex.

Me: You're right. Just no other parts I was *born* to play. *(Dramatically throws hand over eyes.)* So, let me have it. What part did I got?

Stevie: *(Shrugs.)* I don't know, I—I mean, I'm not sure—um, Rosaline?

Me: What do you mean you're not sure? You saw the list.

Joey: *(Chimes in.)* She didn't actually see the list.

Stevie: That's right. I didn't actually see it. I mean, not with my own eyes.

Me: Then, if you didn't see it, maybe you made a mistake. That's it! Maybe you heard wrong or something. This whole thing could be one big melodrama of mishaps, just like in *Romeo and Juliet.*

Joey: (*Blurts.*) Scott Towel told her!

Me: *(Springs to the edge of the bed.)* What! You talked to Scott? What did he say? Sit down. Tell me every single word. Start at the beginning.

Stevie: Well, he came to my homeroom after school. As soon as he saw the Drama Club list and found out he's Romeo—

Me: He's Romeo! I knew it. Just my luck. My life *is* over. Why didn't you tell me?

Stevie: I am telling you. He saw that your name wasn't on the list—

Me: At all? Or just that I'm not Juliet?

Stevie: I don't know. He just really wanted to find you, but he saw me and he was freaking out—

Me: Whoa, whoa. Freaking out how?

Stevie: I don't know. Freaking out.

Joey: Like insane? Foaming at the mouth? Eyes rolling in the back of his head?

Me: Was it freaking out like he likes me and he wishes I got the part? Or freaking out like how is he going to learn all his lines if I'm not there to practice with him?

Stevie: How should I know? All I know is—

Joey: *(Animatedly.)* Jayden Pffeffer got the part! Juliet. Jayden Pffeffer is Juliet. *(Evil eye from Stevie.)*

Me: A plague o' both your houses! They have made worms' meat of me.

Joey: What does that actually mean? *(Whispers to frog.)* Sounds bad.

Me: Jayden Pffeffer? That measle! That toad-spotted maggot! That artless elf-skinned hugger-mugger! I wish she'd shrivel up and turn into a mindless malt-worm. *(Waves Joey and Stevie out the door.)* A glooming peace this morning with it brings. The sun for sorrow will not show his head. Go hence and have more talk of these sad things.

Joey: Huh? *(To Stevie.)* Do you think she wants us to leave?

Stevie: *(Shrugs.)* I guess.

Me: "O woe! O woeful, woeful, woeful day! Most lamentable day. Most woeful day that ever, ever, I did yet behold! O day, O day, O day, O hateful day. Never was seen so black a day as this! O woeful day, O woeful day!"

Joey: What's "woeful"?

Stevie: Let's just put it this way. Not. Good.

1-800-Boy-Calling

Not long after hitting Alex with the bad news, Joey came upstairs and announced, "Mr. Cannon's on the phone." Alex nearly fell off the bed.

"See. I knew it," she said, jabbing a pointed finger at me. "I knew it was all just a big fat mistake."

"Hey, don't look at me. Blame your *boy*friend," I told her.

"He didn't ask for you," said Joey. "He asked to speak with Dad."

"That's weird," Alex said.

I, for one, agreed. "Maybe . . . he wants to ask Dad to borrow some costumes or props, or about the set for *Romeo and Juliet* or something."

"Maybe . . . he wants to ask Dad to direct this time or something," Joey said.

"Yeah! Maybe he didn't pick you for Juliet because Dad will be directing, and that might be weird or something."

"Or maybe . . ." Alex said, holding out hope, "he wants to apologize for making the biggest, giantest mistake of his life. You know, tell Dad he's sorry and ask Dad to tell me."

Joey and I gave each other a look. An I-don't-think-so look.

"Joey. Go downstairs and listen," Alex urged.

"Me? Eavesdrop?" said Joey, faking innocence. Now who's the actress in our family?

Not five minutes later, Joey came racing up the stairs, all out of breath. "The play . . . *Romeo and Juliet* . . ." she said, huffing and puffing. "It's going to be here . . . right here . . . at the Raven!"

All three of us ran downstairs, Alex in the lead. Once Dad was off the phone, she made him explain what was going on.

"With all this rain, they had some kind of a major leak in the school auditorium" said Dad. "The ceiling caved in and flooded the place."

Alex punched me in the arm. "Uh! How could you not tell me this!"

"I didn't know anything about it!" I said.

"It just happened after school today," said Dad. "Mr. Cannon says it'll be a month or more before it'll be dried out and they're allowed back in again."

"So, he wants to use the Raven for play practice?" Alex asked.

"Not just practice," said Dad. "I suggested that we just go ahead and stage the whole thing right here. Isn't that great news, honey?"

"Yeah. Great," Alex mumbled. "Just great."

Dad came over and gave her a hug. "Doing okay, kiddo? I know you had your heart set on playing Juliet. Why didn't you say anything?"

"I just found out myself, Dad. Stevie told me."

"Well, you know what they say. There are no small roles."

"Only small people," Alex chimed in flatly.

"Besides, Nurse isn't exactly a small part. It's the next biggest female role in the—"

"That's the part I got? I'm Nurse? You have *got* to be kidding."

"Who's Nurse? What's so bad about Nurse?" Joey asked.

"See? Nobody even knows who she is! She doesn't

even have a name. Just Juliet's nurse. And she's a bumbling idiot. She's rude and loud and—uh! She's a total fool."

"'O woe! O woeful, woeful, woeful day!'" Dad started in.

"That's Nurse? See, you already know her speech," I said.

"Nurse is an important character, Alex. Some might even argue necessary, because she provides counterpoint to Juliet. You know, comic relief."

Dad was talking like a textbook again. "Arghh!" Alex said. "The only relief would be not being Jayden Pffeffer's nurse!"

"I thought maybe you'd changed your mind and wanted this. Mr. Cannon tells me you pulled off quite a comical audition, and that's what gave him the idea that you'd be perfect for the part of Nurse."

"Great! I was trying for *Juliet.* C'mon, Dad. We both know the only part worse than Nurse is a lowly servant. There's no way I'm taking this part. I'm just going to have to tell Mr. Cannon I quit. Either that, or I'll have to stay home sick for the next two months!"

"On account of the Skittles?" I couldn't help teasing.

"Alex, do you really want to quit the play just because you're not the star?" Dad asked.

In the middle of this heated discussion, the phone on the counter rang again, startling us. Joey picked it up. "Reel residence. Whatcha got for me?" Joey liked to act weird when she answered the phone. Today's personality was Joey Reel, Ace Reporter.

She handed me the phone. "Stevie. For you. It's a *boy.*"

"Ha-ha. Very funny. Gimme." I motioned for her to hand over the phone. I knew it was Olivia.

"Hey," I said, all friendly-like.

"Hey, yourself."

"Excuse me?"

"It's me, Owen. Owen O'Malley. From, um, detention."

"Wire Rims?" I said. It popped out of my mouth before I could stop it.

What in the world was he doing calling me *on the phone*? I took the phone into the family room, away from the owl eyes of my family. I swear my sisters have hearing as sharp as moths.

"Oh. Sorry. Hi." My own voice sounded strange to

me. I'd get Joey back later. "Um . . ." *Stop saying* um! "What's up?" I was talking too fast. "Did you know moths have, like, really great hearing?" I blurted, trying to fill the awkward silence. Great, just great. I sounded like the *Science Friday* guy on the radio.

"I did not know that," said Wire Rims, chuckling. "I didn't think moths had ears."

"Well, ears or not, they're right up there with mice and dolphins. In the hearing department, I mean." Uh! *Stop saying science facts!* Total geekazoid. Why was I talking about *moth ears*?

"Huh. Learn something new every day."

More awkward silence. Was he still there? He's the one who called me. Why wasn't he talking?

"Hello? You still there?" I asked. Why couldn't I just be myself?

"I had a good time today." He speaks!

"At detention?"

"Well, no, not the detention part, but I mean—"

"Oh."

"So, um, you have a little sister too?"

"Yeah."

"How many sisters do you have?"

"Two." What is wrong with me? Whenever this kid talks to me I start speaking in haiku. One-word syllables, anyway. Who's the *boy* here?

"I know it sounds like more. 'Cause they're loud, I mean." *Stop. Don't say your family's fighting or your sister's freaking out or anything.*

"So, what do you say? Say yes."

"Yes. No. I'm sorry, can you repeat the question?" Can you repeat thc question? Have I just lost my mind? This isn't Social Studies class!

"It's about our science labs. You know, the thing where we have to figure out how to simulate a cloud? Mr. Petry said we have to pick a partner, and I was just wondering if maybe you'd be my partner?"

For this, he calls me at home and embarrasses me in front of my whole family? He couldn't just ask me this at school tomorrow?

"I already, um, told Olivia I'd be her partner." Who was I, Pinocchio? The lie just flew out of my mouth. What was wrong with me?

Silence. All I could hear was dead air. Then, "Oh. I thought Olivia wasn't in that class."

"Oh. Right. Yeah. S-sorry," I stuttered, trying to

cover my tracks. "Um, did you say Science? I must have been thinking of Social Studies, where we're definitely going to be partners."

"So, then, you're free? I mean, you'll do it? Be my partner, I mean?"

"Sure, I guess," I said in a fake-excited voice. *What!*

"Really? Are you sure?"

"Why not?" Why not? *Hello!* Because he's a freaking *boy,* that's why not. "I mean, you don't know anybody, seeing as how you're new and everything, and I can't be Olivia's partner, seeing as how she's not in the same class, so this way, everybody would have a partner, except, of course, Olivia, you know?" *Idiot! Shut. Up.*

"Great. Okay. This is *great*! Because I don't know if you knew this about me, but I have volcanophobia."

"Fear of volcanoes?"

"More like fear of science projects. A volcano blew up on me in the third grade. Let's just say I added too much baking soda. And *way* too much red food coloring. I've never been the same."

"That sounds a lot like the Great Kool-Aid Disaster of '07. I spilled, like, a whole can of green powder, and when I tried to wipe it up so my mom wouldn't find out, well, let's just say I turned the entire kitchen neon green and my mom wasn't too happy with me." My voice sounded almost normal now.

"So, is it safe to say green is *not* your favorite color?"

I giggled like a goofus. And just like that, I was talking to a *boy.*

Ten Ways Stevie Is Acting (Too Much) Like Alex
by Joey Reel

1. Got detention.
2. Boys calling (one boy, anyway).
3. Looks in mirror a lot.
4. Looks in Alex's room a lot.
5. Doesn't read to me anymore.
6. Takes super long in the bathroom.
7. Wants her hair to grow back.
8. Burns favorite troll doll from childhood.
9. Is not grossed-out enough when Alex talks about kissing.

Okay, so, there are only nine. But still!

Joey Reel, Propmaster

The play is going to be here! At the Raven! Right next door! Dad says I can help collect props and even make some of them with him.

List of Props in Romeo and Juliet:

- sonnet book
- hand bell
- paper lanterns
- rope ladder
- 2 knives, 1 dagger
- tons of ivy (fake or real?)
- poison bottle
- music box
- 3 white sheets
- ton of pearls (white beads?)
- 2 ribbon lockets
- fan
- fancy hankies
- walking stick

- giant feather
- flashlights
- masks
- drum
- red rose

Alex gave me a sonnet book to use. Mom had some old-fashioned embroidered hankies. And Stevie helped me find a really good jaggedy walking stick. Dad says I can help make the masks they wear to the ball. And the rope of pearls Juliet wears like a belt around her dress. YAYYYYYY!

KISS BUSTER

Starring Alex

SETTING: ALEX'S ROOM, A FEW DAYS LATER . . .

Me: Emergency meeting of the Sisters Club! My room. Stat.

Joey: What's up?

Me: What's up? My life is a complete and total disaster, that's what's up.

Stevie: Alex, everything with you is always a Drama-Queen disaster.

Me: But this time it really is! First of all, I had to tell Mr. Cannon I quit the play. Second of all, they're over there practicing—right next door—right now! Hello! I live here!

Joey: What? Wait, you quit the play?

Stevie: You can't just quit the play.

Me: I know. But I did.

Stevie: What did Mr. Cannon say when you told him?

Me: Let's just say he went all Hamlet on me.

Joey: Not happy?

Me: Hardly. I mean, it's bad enough that I don't get to be Juliet. And Jayden Pffeffer does! So I quit and what happens? They start practicing here every single day! I thought it would just be over if I quit. How am I going to hide? There's no escape!

Stevie: So?

Joey: So?

Me: *So?* Don't you get it? Scott Towel, I mean Scott Howell, is right next door!

Joey: But you like him, right?

Me: Duh. Way to state the obvious. Yes, I like him.

Stevie: *(Nods in agreement.)* So, it should be a good thing that he's practicing here, right? Because you'll get to see him every day even though you're not going to be in the play.

Me: Wrong! The *plan* was for him to be Romeo. The *plan* was for *me* to be Juliet. The *plan* was for us to have our first kiss. The *plan* was for it to be totally romantic, just like in *Romeo and Juliet.* But now, the *plan* is totally and completely screwed up, thanks to one Miss Jayden Fluffernutter, a.k.a Queen Aggravating.

Joey: *(Cracks up.)* Oh.

Stevie: *Oh!*

Me: Is that all you guys have to say? "Oh"?

Joey: *(Chants.)* Alex and Scott Towel, sitting in a tree. K-I-S-S-I-N-G!

Me: *(Ignores Joey.)* C'mon, people. I need a plan. A brand-new plan. A brand-new, brilliant plan. You have to help me. I'm going crazy!

Stevie: What kind of plan?

Joey: A man plan. *(Cracks herself up.)*

Stevie: Alex, you know you want to be in the play. So just go over there and UN-quit.

Alex: Okay, I admit, maybe I do kind of wish I hadn't freaked out and quit. But I can't just un-quit now. So, here's the thing. I need to know everything that goes on over there, but since I'm not in the play, I can't just hang around for no reason.

Joey: Pretend you have to ask Dad something.

Stevie: Or pretend you left something over there.

Me: Too lame. They'll be onto me in, like, two seconds flat.

Stevie: But . . . they won't be onto Joey!

Joey: Huh?

Stevie: You said you were going to help Dad with the *Romeo and Juliet* props and sets.

Joey: Yeah, Dad says we can build a balcony with a rope ladder and everything. But I'll be painting and stuff. In the back. I can't just hang around all day waiting to see if Scott Towel kisses some girl. It's gross. And boring.

Me: C'mon, Joey. This is super important. Scott could be over there kissing Fluffernutter right this very minute.

Joey: *Gross!* You know kissing is just spit, right? *(Makes saliva bubbles with her mouth.)* One person's spit goes into another person's mouth and it's super disgusting. Like, a ten on the Grossometer. I mean, you wouldn't go around using Scott Towel's *toothbrush,* would you?

Me: No, but this is different. You don't get it, Duck. But someday you will.

Stevie: You know, Joey. It might be kind of . . . interesting. Like a super-secret stakeout.

Joey: Well, all I'm saying is find someone else. I'm not going to be your Kiss Buster. I wish nobody would kiss anybody around here.

Stevie: Wait a second. I might have an idea. Hold on, I'll be right back *(Runs upstairs to attic, clomps back down. Hides something behind her back.)*

Me: What? What is it?

Stevie: Ta-da! It's Joey's old baby monitor.

You know, you turn it on and you can hear if the baby is crying from downstairs. I saw it up in the attic one day when I was cloudspotting.

Me: Brilliant! Does it have video?

Stevie: Not that brilliant. Just audio.

Me: Never mind. All we need are batteries and someone to sneak over there and plant it in the exact right place.

Joey: Don't look at me!

Me: C'mon, Duck, you love this stuff. It'll be cool. You'll be like an undercover spy.

Stevie: It'll be very *croak*-and-dagger. Get it, Joey? *(Slaps her knee and cracks up.)*

Me: Yeah, like that guy Christopher Marlowe in Shakespeare's time. I think he got murdered, though. But there were tons of spies back then.

Stevie: We can even give you a cool title, like Her Royal Spyness.

Me: That's way better than just being a royal pain.

Joey: I don't know . . . maybe. But who

wants to hear people kissing? Yuck. What kind of a spy is that?

Me: A kissing spy.

Joey: There's no such thing. Anyway, that's cuckoo. Tell her, Stevie.

Stevie: I don't know, Joey. It might be kind of interesting to, I don't know, hear what it's like when they ki—I mean, hear what they say. Think of it like a mystery. And you're spying to try to solve a mystery.

Joey: Mystery? What mystery? The mystery of boys. Bluck.

Me: Look. All *you* have to do is take the baby monitor over there and hide it. You don't even have to listen if you don't want to.

Joey: But what if they see me? What do I say I'm doing? Or what if Dad finds it and gets mad about spying or something?

Me: He won't. Not if you hide it. Besides, there's so many props and stuff over there, how's he going to know? C'mon, Duck. Please? I'll do anything. Just name it.

Joey: Oh, okay.

Me: You mean it? You'll do it?

Joey: Yes. But only if you promise to really call me Her Royal Spyness for one whole entire day. *And* give me twenty-five dollars.

Me: Deal! Except for the twenty-five dollars part.

Thespianage

Alex and I were kneeling on my bed with our faces pressed to the second-story window. "Stop breathing so much," I told her. "You're fogging up the window and I can't see."

I wiped the altocumulus cloud Alex had made on the window with the side of my fist. "There she is!" Alex pointed at Joey, a.k.a. Her Royal Spyness, sneaking up on the side of the Raven Theater next door to our house.

"What's she wearing?" Alex asked, craning her neck.

"A raincoat?" I said, straining to see.

"But it's not even raining, for once." The sky was overcast, but the drizzle had stopped.

"Don't you get it? It's a spy thing." We watched Joey reach into her pocket. She put on a pair of dark sunglasses. And a Sherlock Holmes houndstooth hat with earflaps from Dad's props trunk. "All she needs now is a pipe."

"Um, wrong century, Joey," Alex pretended to call out, even though Joey couldn't hear her. "I don't think Shakespeare spies knew about Sherlock Holmes."

"Never mind. Joey gets to be a spy. And you get to eavesdrop on Scott Towel. It's win-win." I grinned at my sister. It's not like I'm into kissing—I felt pretty much like Joey did about it, high up on the Grossometer. But I have to admit, I was a little curious. It's not every day you get to spy on two people when they're going to kiss. A strange prickle set the hairs on the back of my neck on end.

"Yeah, but now if anybody sees her they're going to know she's a spy."

Just then, Joey bent down and duckwalked along the side of the building, hunching beneath the windows. The monitor crackled. "Testing. Testing. I'm outside the theater. I'm almost to the back door."

Just then her hat fell off.

"Let it go, Joey. Just let it go," Alex willed her out loud.

Joey disappeared around the back of the theater until we couldn't see her any more.

"What's that sound?" I asked.

"It's probably just the creaking of the back steps."

"I'm on the back stairs," Joey reported.

"She's in!" I said proudly.

"She better stop reporting her every move. They'll hear her. And I'll be busted before I even get to spy on Scott and Jayden."

"Shh. Who's that?" I asked, motioning for my sister to be quiet.

Dad.

"Hi, honey." *Rustle, rustle.* "Everything okay?" *Clank, clank, clank.* "I'm just sorting through a bunch of old props for *Romeo and Juliet.* I have swords, a dagger, a vial of poison, a bunch of grapes . . . but I can't find that dozen roses with the dew on it, and this wedding cake, I think, will have to be painted." *Crackle, crackle.* "It's looking a bit shabby, don't you think?"

"Sure, Dad."

"So, what brings you over?"

"Um . . . I am here . . . um . . . because . . ."

"Just say anything, Joey," my sister urged, even though Joey couldn't hear her. "It doesn't matter if it's lame. Say something."

"I'm not spying or anything," said Joey.

"Joey!" Alex put her head in her hand. "I give up," she said to me.

"Don't worry. Dad's hardly listening. I can still hear him rifling through stuff. There's, like, a million boxes in that props closet."

"Stevie, um, asked me to come over. Not Alex. Alex didn't ask me. Yep. It was Stevie."

"Me?" I exclaimed. "Thanks a lot. Don't go blaming me, little sister."

"Uh-huh," said Dad, still half listening. "What did she want?"

"She, um, she, well, she . . . made you a sandwich!"

What!

"Great. What kind?"

"What kind? Technically, I'm not sure."

"Doesn't matter. I'll take it, whatever it is."

"You know, funny thing is, I forgot to bring it over. So, I'm just going to go back over there, to the house

I mean, and get it. And then I'll come back over here. So, I'll be back."

"Are you sure you're okay?" Dad.

"I'm sure. I'm just going to go now."

"Okay, I'll just be a little while longer, if anybody needs me, you know where to find me. I'll wait till they're done practicing in here and then I'll lock up."

"Can I go out there, Dad?"

"Not today, honey. I don't think Mr. Cannon would like us interrupting practice."

"How about if . . . can I just take a peek from backstage? I'll stay behind the curtain."

"Sure. I don't see why not."

Silence. More rustling. More crackling.

Alex held up the monitor and we glued our ears to it, trying to hear. But all we could hear was a lot of rustling and clomping and crackling and static.

Somebody coughed.

"What's happening now? Do you think it died?" asked Alex.

"It didn't die," I told her. "I just heard a cough."

"What cough? Who coughed? Was it a guy cough?" Alex asked.

"How should I know a guy cough from a girl cough?"

"Well, you know, was it deep like a man teacher's do you think? Or was it just, you know, *heh-heh,* like a younger person?"

"You're seriously warped, you know that."

"Why can't we hear anything? It's not working. Do you think Joey bumped it? Or turned it off or something? What if she put it behind the curtain, like I told her, and now we can't hear."

"Take a chill pill. Just wait till Joey gets back. She'll tell us what's going on."

Alex started biting her fingernails. I pulled her hand away and she stuck her tongue out at me.

"This is so cool," I said. "It's kind of like that Hitchcock movie."

"The one where they have a chase scene on Mount Rushmore?" she asked. "Or the one where millions of birds attack people? Wait, it's the one where the creepy guy has a skeleton in the basement, huh?"

"*Psycho*? You're psycho. I meant the one where the guy is holed up in this room in a wheelchair. All he does is stare out the window all day. And he thinks he sees a murderer in the building next door. So he sends somebody over there to find out."

"The only murder around here is going to be Joey's if she doesn't get back here soon."

Just then, Joey Reel, Her Royal Spyness, burst into the room with a mud-streaked face and a hole in her jeans.

"What happened to you?" I asked.

"Stevie. Hurry. Quick. You have to make Dad a sandwich!"

Off with Her Head!
by Joey Reel

There were tons of spies and secret codes in Shakespeare's time. I read about them in this book Alex has about all the crazy queens back then.

Guess what? When Elizabeth was queen, she was like, "Go to your room" and locked up her cousin Mary for nineteen years. But Mary smuggled some notes out of prison. They were written in secret code. And the notes said she had a plan to kill the queen!

Don't think Queen Elizabeth didn't have her own spies. She was even better at espionage (fancy word for spying). Her spies stole the notes and cracked the secret code! Elizabeth was so mad, she said, "Off with her head!" Here's the real code:

A	B	C	D	E	F	G	H	I	K	L	M	N	O	P	Q	R	S	T	U	X	Y	Z
0	ǂ	Λ	⧻	a	□	θ	∞	l	ŏ	n	//	ø	∇	s	m	f	∆	ε	c	7	8	9

I bet you are wondering what happened to the letters J, V, and W. So was I! It's weird, but back then, a letter I was the same as a J, and U and V were the same, too. Don't ask me about W!

Here's a secret message I wrote in super-spy code to Alex:

ŧalØθ O ▵s8 |▵ Ɛ▿ƐOnn8 Λ▿▿n.
∞OØ⧻ ▿caf //8 //▿Øa8!

To Woo, Perchance to Smooch

It had been three days. Three days of listening in on play practice with the baby monitor. Three days of watching Alex mouth the words as Scott Towel and Jayden struggled through their lines.

Joey yawned. "Why do they call it eavesdropping? Why not ears-dropping? My ears are dropping off. Even kissing would not be this boring."

"Shh! Joey! I can't hear," said Alex.

"So? All they ever do is go, 'perchance, perforce, blah-blah. Anon! Anon!'"

"Yeah, how come we never get to hear Scott Towel and Jayden say stuff to each other?" I asked.

"Un-Shakespeare stuff, I mean." I could hear Shakespeare anytime, but I never got to spy on a boy and girl talking before.

"Because they're practicing for a play? How should I know? Maybe they talk to each other all the time, but they don't stand near the baby monitor. Maybe they have Pianophobia. Shush, you guys. I mean it."

Alex flipped through her script book. "It's the party scene at Juliet's house. They're in Act 1 Scene 5. Mr. Cannon only has two kisses in *Romeo and Juliet* and this scene has one of them. And this is the one where Juliet's not dead."

We could hear Scott Towel's voice say, "My lips, two blushing pilgrims, ready stand, To smooch that rough touch with a tender kiss."

"Smooch? He said 'smooch.' Was he supposed to say 'smooch'?" I asked.

Alex rubbed her forehead like it hurt her head to listen. "No, it's 'smooth.' Smooth. I don't know why he's messing up like this."

"Good pilgrim, your hand is wrong, wait, good pilgrim, your wrong hand is, uh! I give up," we heard Jayden say.

"Good pilgrim, you do wrong your hand too much!" said an exasperated Alex. "What's so hard about that?"

"Everything," said Joey.

"How can they screw this up so bad?" Alex asked. "This is a disaster. Even Scott keeps messing up. Can't anybody in Drama Club act anymore?"

"The Nurse is funny," said Joey.

"Yeah, she's the only good one. And that was supposed to be my part. What is my problem? Maybe I should have stuck it out."

"Maybe it's not too late," I suggested. "Maybe there's still a part—"

"Shh!" said Alex. "Mr. Cannon's yelling. I want to hear."

"People, people. What is going on today? Scott, your delivery's flat. Jayden, you're tripping over your own tongue. You could try practicing simple tongue twisters. It's a great vocal warm-up exercise to help with Shakespeare."

"But I don't even get what half of it means." Jayden.

"Sure you do. Romeo is laying eyes on Juliet for the

first time. I'm sure you've heard of love at first sight? He's blown away by her beauty. He feels unworthy of her love. Let the feelings come, and the words will follow."

"But why does she call him a pilgrim? Did they even have Thanksgiving back then? And why does she keep talking about hands and stuff?" Jayden again.

Mr. Cannon. "'For saints have hands that pilgrims' hands do touch, And palm to palm is holy palmers' kiss.' Now you try. Don't look at the script right now. Just try to feel the words inside you."

"For saints have hands like pilgrims, palm by palm by palm holy kiss."

"Let's move on. I want to get to the end of this scene. Romeo? Have not saints lips."

Alex mouthed the words, motioning to us to keep quiet. Scott Towel. "Have not saints lips, and holy palmers, too?"

"Ay, pilgrim, lips that they must use in prayer," Alex whispered, her eyes closed.

"Ay, pilgrim, lips that they must use in . . . Ping-Pong?" Jayden.

"You should have been Juliet," said Joey. "Not her."

"Take five, people. We'll pick it back up with Benvolio."

"Oh holy of holies," said Joey, imitating Juliet. "Kiss thy pilgrim hand and smooch thy pilgrim lips."

"Even Joey is better than Jayden," I said.

Just then, the monitor crackled and the voices got louder. "Shh! It's them!" said Alex. "Scott and Jayden! They must be standing right next to the monitor."

"I hope they don't look behind the curtain," said Joey.

"My fault? All I did was say 'smooch.'" Scott.

"Yeah, no wonder I was thrown off." Jayden.

"My bad. I make one mistake. You're not even making sense." Scott.

"Can I help it if Juliet talks in tongue twisters?" Jayden again.

"You're supposed to read all your lines the night before so this doesn't happen. We sound like idiots out there. I don't know why Mr. Cannon . . ." His voice trailed off.

"Why Mr. Cannon what?" Alex practically screamed.

"Oh, don't even go there. Look, I'm Juliet. Not her." Jayden.

"Who her?" Scott.

"She's talking about me!" said Alex.

"Alex Reel. Who else?" Jayden.

Alex turned to look at me, her eyes wide as dinner plates.

"Hey. This isn't about her." Scott.

"Oh, isn't it? Little Miss Woe Is Me I Can't Be in the Play If I'm Not the Lead. She's been the lead in every play since, like, the third grade." Jayden.

"Second grade," said Alex.

"At least Alex Reel takes it seriously. At least she knows her lines. Look. Just forget her, okay?" Scott.

"I will if you will."

"What a snot," said Alex. "Go back to *The Princess Diaries,*" she called.

"Who says—" Scott Towel.

"Oh, come on. Don't even try to lie. You wish Alex got the part, don't you? Just say it." Jayden.

Silence. Static.

"Say yes, say yes," said Alex, crossing her fingers.

"Well, I'm sick of her! 'Ooh, I'm so pretty with my

big green eyes' and 'Ooh, I'm so into Shakespeare' and 'Ooh, I've known all the lines since I was, like, four.' Well, guess what? Mr. Cannon didn't pick her. He picked me. Deal with it." Jayden.

Alex leaned back on her feet. "I so do not sound like that," she said.

Crackle, crackle. Static. White noise.

Alex shook the monitor. "Hey, what's happening to this thing? Don't break on me now."

"Yeah, *crackle,* well, *crackle,* that was in a lake." Scott.

"And guess what else? You're going to be kissing me, Romeo, *not* Alex Reel." Jayden.

The monitor crackled again.

"We'll cheese a snack." Scott.

Joey looked at me. I looked at Joey. We both looked at Alex. "Did he just say 'that was in a lake'?" I asked.

"And 'we'll cheese a snack'?" Joey asked. Joey and I busted up laughing. I snorted, and Joey held her sides like they hurt.

"I hope he said, 'That was a mistake.' You know, like he thinks picking Jayden was a mistake. And the second part was, maybe, 'I'll be right back.' No wait, I think it was, 'We'll see about that.'"

"Wow," Joey said. "You're like a master spy who cracked the code."

"Yeah," I said to Alex. "Who knew? You speak Scott Towel!"

Tongue Twisters
(Without the Sisters and Blisters)
by Joey Reel

I heard Mr. Cannon tell Jayden that she should practice tongue twisters to help her recite Shakespeare better. Here are some good ones for her. (Shh! Don't tell Alex, the green-eyed monster!)

Which witch wished which wish?
A noisy noise annoys an oyster.
Kindly kittens knitting mittens keep
  kazooing in the king's kitchen.
A Tudor who tooted a flute tried to
  tutor two Tudors to toot.

HEY!
Juliet Jayden
does not deserve
jolly jingles! A.

Here are some I made up:

Alex the actress astonished an astronaut.

Stevie cooks chocolate cupcakes quickly.

Joey juggles jiggly Jell-O while jumping jump rope.

A three-toed tree toad kissed a two-toed she-toad. A.

The two-toed she-toad vetoed the three-toed tree toad ~S

Hey! MY notebook. No kissing allowed! —J

Too bad for you. Tongue twister is also a name for a kiss. A.

BLUUUUUUCKKKKKKKK! Why didn't you tell me? —J

Girl in Black

On Saturday, I came downstairs from reading in bed till almost noon, my favorite weekend thing. It's rare in our house to have a quiet Saturday morning, and usually Joey jumps on my bed, waking me up by eight o'clock. (Unless Sir Croaks-a-Lot beats her to it.) Today, I hated to leave the warmth of the covers.

I thought I smelled something cooking . . . or was it burning? Maybe it was just the wintry smell of wood smoke from neighboring chimneys. Whatever it was, it did not smell like breakfast.

In the kitchen, Mom had zucchini littered all over the table and countertops and she was talking out loud to herself.

"What's with the zucchini factory, Mom?"

"Stevie, honey, I'm so glad you're here. I need your help."

"Where is everybody?"

"They're all next door at the theater. Something about a trap door in the floor? Dad wanted to show Joey, and Alex went too."

"So you started talking to zucchini?"

"Of course not. Just thinking aloud. I'm trying to come up with a recipe for next week's show. They want me to do a show on healthy foods for kids. So I'm working on a way to get kids to eat zucchini."

"You're going to need a magician to get kids to eat zucchini, Mom. The Nutrition Magician!" I couldn't help cracking up at my own joke.

"The Nutrition Magician?"

"Don't ask. He came to our school to give an assembly. It's a long story."

"Well, I'm no magician, but I thought I'd try out a recipe for zucchini-crust pizza. But as you can see, this one came out with a lake in the middle—see how soggy it is? And this one fell apart completely."

Mom exhaled loudly, wiping her hands down the

sides of her jeans and plopping into a chair. "I just have to sit for a minute. Would you mind grating the rest of this zucchini?"

My mom is an actress turned chef. A.k.a. Fondue Sue. She has a cooking show (even though she's the world's worst cook). She recently graduated from Hamburger Helper to Tuna Helper, but it still tasted like tofu. And her chicken Kiev, well, let's just say it should go back to Ukraine.

I started grating.

"So, what's new, kiddo?" Mom asked.

I paused. "Is this about detention?" I asked.

"Did I say detention?" Mom asked, holding up her hands defensively.

"Mom, don't worry. It was no big deal. Honest. Olivia and I were just trying to be nice to some new kid, but we weren't supposed to be talking during an assembly." *Grr.* Grate, grate, grate.

"Well, that's good of you two. What's her name?"

"Um . . . well . . . actually, it's a him."

"A him, huh?" Mom said teasingly.

"It's *not* like that! Why does everybody—never mind." I pushed down on the zucchini and grated my knuckle instead. A little bubble of blood appeared.

"Youch. That hurt," I said, sucking on my thumb to stop the bleeding.

"Sorry. I didn't mean to tease. I didn't realize this was a sensitive topic. I know this is a tough age, honey, but—"

"Mom. Spare me. Not the 'tough age' speech. Can we just *please* not talk about this!" Sheesh. What was wrong with me? I was beginning to sound like Alex. And I was supposed to be the normal one. Middle child. Peacemaker.

"So. Any ideas for my zucchini pizza?" Mom asked, changing the subject.

"Maybe press all of the water out of the zucchini before you mix it up into the crust? And I would bake the crust by itself first, so it hardens, before you put the sauce and cheese and stuff on it."

"Good idea. I'll try that."

"Maybe turn the oven up, too. To four fifty?"

"Okay. Got it. Thanks."

Done grating, I set the grater down. There was an awkward pause, where the room felt too quiet.

"Well, I better go get a Band-Aid for my thumb."

"Are you sure everything's okay, honey?" Mom asked.

"I'm sure," I said, even though inside I felt a little shaky.

Upstairs, the house was quiet. It was rare to have the house (almost) to myself. I walked past Alex's room on my way to the medicine cabinet. I paused, listened. Just familiar kitchen sounds, of Mom opening cupboards, running water, clinking dishes.

Without thinking, I ducked into Alex's room and hurried over to her dresser. Before I even realized what I was doing, I yanked open the third drawer, rifled through her pile of T-shirts, and dug out the black shirt. The one. The one Joey and I had discovered the other day.

Grabbing the shirt, I peered out the doorway of her room, looking both ways down the hallway to make sure the coast was clear. Then I quickly rushed into my room and shut the door.

I yanked off the LIFE'S A BEACH shirt I wear to sleep in, unfolded the other, and pulled it over my head. What was I doing?

I couldn't help myself. I wanted to see it in the bathroom mirror. But what if Alex came back and found me out? I pulled my fuzzy robe off the hook and put it on over the shirt, dashed down the hall into the bathroom, and locked the door.

I took off the robe. Turned on the light. Stared at myself in the mirror.

The Girl in Black.

A basket of tub toys from when we were little still sat on the corner shelf over the radiator. Purple hippo. Toy boat. Mostly Joey's old rubber ducky collection. It seemed like forever ago since Joey and I had taken baths, drawing with crayons on the tub walls.

An army of blue, green, and red devil duckies with horns stared at me accusingly.

"What are you looking at?" I said aloud. "I should have burned you in the fire," I told the red one. So there.

I tugged at my hair, brushed my bangs down almost over my eyes. I turned to the left, turned to the right, looking at myself from every angle—front, side, other side. I made pouty-lips. I made a tough-girl face.

I hardly recognized myself.

Who was this girl who stared back at me in the bluish bright light of the bathroom?

Is this what it felt like to try out for a role in a play, to get to be somebody else? To imagine yourself as other than what you were?

Is this what it felt like to be Alex?

To be grown up? A teenager? Someone who liked boys?

My pulse quickened. I felt secret and alone. I felt a little bit daring, like the kind of girl you'd find in Bad-Girl Detention.

A knock on the bathroom door made me jump out of my skin.

"Stevie? Are you in there? Can you come out so I can ask you a question?"

Holy tamale! Mom!

I cast around, looking for my robe, threw it back on over the shirt, tied the belt, and opened the door.

"What's up?" I asked, trying to sound nonchalant.

"Stevie? What are you wearing?" Mom asked pointedly.

I clasped the collar of the bathrobe together with one hand. What . . . how . . . Had she seen?

"Honey, are you sure everything's okay? What are you doing in your bathrobe in the middle of the day?

It's almost one o'clock. Don't you want to go over to the theater with the others? What's Olivia doing today?"

"Mom—you had a question?"

"How many eggs do you think I should use to hold the crust together?"

"How about if I come down and help you?" I suggested sweetly. "Just give me two minutes."

One minute to put the shirt back where it belonged. Hidden. Safe.

And one minute to come back to being Stevie again.

Reel Math

by Joey Reel

- # of pearls I had to string for Juliet's belt: 197!
- # of feathers I glued on Romeo's mask: 36
- # of times Alex and I went through the trap door: 13, at least
- # of zucchinis Mom had in the kitchen: 10 trillion
- # of zucchini pizzas Mom made: 10
- # of zucchini pizzas that were edible: NOT 10; 2
- # of times Alex says she wishes she could be Juliet: 1 million
- # of times Alex did not complain about Jayden: 0
- # of times Dad quoted Shakespeare in one day: 9
- # of clouds Stevie glued to her poster so far: 22
- # of times Sir-Croaks-a-Lot got out this week: 3
- # of times Stevie acted like Alex this week: 2½
- # of times I have seen Alex wear The Shirt: 0

Furious Yellow

Sunlight streamed through the windows of Mr. Petry's classroom, casting the whole room in a curious yellow. It had been sunshiny now for three days in a row, but I still felt myself squinting in the bright light after so many days of gloom. Mom said this morning it was like breaking free of a Dickens novel.

On Thursday, Earth Science was half over when Mr. Petry pulled a fast one. Passing out worksheets on the scientific method, he said, "For the remainder of class, I want you to buddy up with your partner. You have ten or fifteen minutes to discuss your weather experiments."

Moans and groans rippled through the classroom.

"Start with your question, form a hypothesis, and fill in the worksheet. What's your best guess as to the outcome? Don't forget to add sections on gathering materials, observations, and data. Projects are due next week, people."

Wire Rims dragged his chair over to my desk, sitting a little too close. He had on a gray thermal under a black shirt with a troll doll(!) on it.

We hunched over the worksheet. "So, what's our hypothesis?" *Why are you wearing a troll doll shirt? How weird is that?* "We have to think up a question that we're going to answer."

"Okay, well, we're going to do the cloud thing, right? The one I told you about that we did at my old school? We use ice and hot water and *poof*! It forms a cloud. It's really cool. And it'll be super easy since I've done it before." He glanced up front to make sure Mr. Petry didn't hear that part.

"Ice and water," I said, writing it under "Gather Materials."

"Write that down. Under 'Gather Materials'."

"Very funny," I told him. He leaned back, looking pleased with himself. "Okay. Hypothesis . . . What makes a cloud form? How does a cloud form? What are the conditions that bring about a cloud?"

"Hypothesis: You like that band the Notebooks," he said.

"Huh? Hello. This isn't music class."

"But you're into them, aren't you? Am I right or am I right? Just say it. You're into the Notebooks."

"Okay. I'm into the Notebooks. The *science* notebooks," I said, jabbing the worksheet with my pencil.

Observation: Wire Rims was not taking this project seriously.

"Are you into their new song—what's it called? 'Honey Strange.' Or is it 'Honey Stranger'?"

"You're strange. And getting stranger by the second."

"I just thought—their lead singer, Chloe Sevilla, has that cool haircut. Short, you know, with bangs in her eyes. Kinda like yours."

My hand shot up to my hair. "Trust me, this short hair was not on purpose. Long story."

"I'd like to hear it sometime."

Secretly I liked that he wanted to hear my hair-disaster story. But that would have to wait for later.

"Can we please stop talking about my hair? We still don't have a hypothesis."

"No biggie. I told you, I got it covered. Piece of cake."

"So I should write 'piece of cake'?" I teased. "Where exactly do you want me to put that?"

"Ha, ha. What other bands are you into? Me, I'm into everything from old-school Beatles and Dylan to indie bands like the Troll Dolls and Furious Yellow."

"Hey, Wire Rims. Can we focus here? Before Mr. Petry turns furious yellow."

Wire Rims cracked up. "Hey, that's funny."

I couldn't help grinning. "Shh. Do you want to end up in detention again?"

"Might not be so bad."

"Let's talk about materials," I said for the benefit of Mr. Petry. "What else, besides water and ice?"

Mr. Petry moved on to the next row.

"I'm way into music." Wire Rims drummed a beat on top of my desk. "Okay, this is so cool. For my report, you know, the cloud identification thing? I'm even identifying how many times the word 'cloud' appears in certain music, like Dylan. And if I have time, I'll do rain, thunder, and lightning, too."

"How'd you think of that? That sounds cool! But we haven't even filled out—" The bell rang before I could finish my sentence. "Saved by the bell," I said. "So, what time on Saturday? And where do you want to meet? The library?"

"No way can we do this at the library! I mean, there's ice, and we have to use hot water and stuff. I know. You can come to my house. It's not that far from the school. You turn at that pink house that used to be a video store."

No way was I going over to his house! Too weird. "Look. You know where the Raven Theater is, right off Main Street South? I live right next door. Why don't you just meet me there? It'll be easier."

"I'll bring ice. You bring water," he said, smiling and showing off a crooked front tooth.

"How about if I bring water and *you* bring ice?"

"Wait," he said, shaking his head. "Isn't that what I just said?"

"Gotcha." Now it was my turn to smile.

Draw Conclusions: Cloudy, with a chance of flunking Earth Science.

GOT FOG?

Starring Alex

SETTING: ALEX'S ROOM, THE NEXT AFTERNOON.

Me: Joey, you have to go over there again. You heard them yesterday. Mr. Cannon is going to make them do the same scene today. And they're going to have to get it right. That means they're going to kiss . . . more than once. You have to stop them!

Joey: No way, nah-uh, not me.

Me: Stevie?

Stevie: *(Imitates Joey.)* No way, no how, nah-uh.

Me: *(Wails.)* C'mon, you guys. You have to help me. When have I ever asked you for anything?

Joey and Stevie: *(At same time.)* Yesterday.

Stevie: Alex, what is the big deal? So they kiss. It's just a play. They're acting.

Me: Yeah, acting like they like each other.

At first, you're just pretending, then, *boom,* you're in love.

Stevie: Just go over there. So what if you're not in the play. You can't hide up here forever. Joey and I are going to take the baby monitor away, aren't we, Joey? *(Signals to Joey to grab it.)*

Me: You can't. *(Grabs it back.)* Okay, I'll go, but—

Joey: Dad's over there. Just say he needs some help with props.

Me: Thank you.

Stevie: Go. Remember, we'll be right here! *(Shakes baby monitor in air.)*

Me: *(Runs out door and across to Raven Theater. Enters through back door.)*

Mr. Cannon: Hi, stranger! What do you think of our new digs? *(Gestures all around theater.)*

Jayden: *(Under her breath, but still heard.)* What's she doing here? I thought she was too good for us now.

Scott: Alex!

Allen/Alvin: Hi, Alex.

Conrad/Matt/Brianna: Hey, Alex.

Me: My dad told me you guys were rehearsing here. Sorry to hear about the school theater flooding and everything.

Matt: This place is cool.

Mr. Cannon: *(A little too cheery.)* Well, sure was great of your dad to let us use the space. And I was hoping we'd run into you. We miss seeing you at Drama Club.

Me: Um, yeah, thanks, me too, but . . . don't let me interrupt. I'm not staying or anything. It's just, my dad asked me to come over and look over some props. Help figure out what we're missing and everything. You know.

Jayden: Yeah, right.

Mr. Cannon: That's great, Alex.

Me: So, just forget I'm here.

Jayden: *(Mutters.)* That shouldn't be hard.

Scott: *(Glares at Jayden.)*

Me: I'll be in the back. I'll try not to make

noise. I know you guys must have a lot to do. *(Looks directly at Jayden.)*

Allen/Alvin: Sure do.

Me: I mean a lot of work. Practice. I know. I get it. *(Stop talking now!)*

Mr. Cannon: *(Claps hands.)* Okay, people. Can I have Romeo, Juliet, Nurse, Benvolio, and a Capulet. Front and center. Let's hit it. I want to get through Act One today. Juliet!

Jayden: My only love sprung from my only hate.

Scott: That's not even the line, Mr. Cannon.

Mr. Cannon: Juliet, take it from "Good pilgrim."

Jayden: Fine. Good pilgrim, you do wrong your hand too much

Mr. Cannon: With expression.

Me: *(Listens from behind the curtain.)*

Scott: Have not saints lips, and holy palmers, too?

Me: *(Whispers into monitor.)* Hey, guys. It's me. Alex. We forgot one thing. I'm over here, but, I mean, how do I keep the kiss from happening? *(Oh, yeah, they can hear me, but I can't hear them.)* They're doing the scene! Close your ears, Joey. It's coming up in, like, two seconds. *(Rummages through props. Looks around backstage. Ladder. Fan. Guitar. Maybe I can drop something, make a loud crash. Aren't there any trash cans back here? Chairs?)*

Scott: O then, dear saint, let lips do what hands do.

Me: *(Eyes land on fog machine.)* Hey, guys. I have a great idea. *(Hurry up! Plug it in! Aim nozzle of hose through gap in curtain. Wait for Scott to say "prayer's effect I take.")*

Scott: Then move not while my prayer's effect I take.

Me: *(Now! Turns switch to ON. Blast of fog gushes onto the stage.)*

Jayden: Uh! My eyes! *(Holds hands up to shield face.)* I can't see! *(Waves hand in* *front of her face, rubs hands across both eyes. Coughs.)* Mr. Cannon, she did this on purpose!

Me: *(Pokes head through gap in curtain.)* Sorry. I was just testing the fog machine for my dad.

Mr. Cannon: Settle down, people. No harm done. Well, at least we know it's working. That fog'll come in handy for the graveyard scene. Okay, Juliet. Your line. "You kiss by the book."

Jayden: *(Overdramatizes a cough.)* You kiss . . . *ahem, ahem* . . . by the . . . *ahem* . . . book.

Mr. Cannon: Benvolio, away, begone. Everybody exit but Juliet and Nurse. Jayden, Come hither, Nurse.

BACKSTAGE, MOMENTS LATER . . .

Scott: Oh, my god, Alex, did you see her face? *(Laughs.)* That was too funny. Then she wiped her eyes and they smudged all black, like raccoon eyes. *(Lowers voice* *and imitates.)* Hey, Jayden. Got fog? *Pffffff!*

Me: I didn't mean to get you, honest!

Scott: It was worth it. Getting fogged, I mean. Just to see the Jayden freak-out. I don't know what's up with her. She's freaking out all over the place.

Me: Really?

Scott: Yeah, like yesterday. You shoulda heard her.

Me: *(Innocently.)* Yeah, I wish I could have.

Scott: We're at the end of Act One, right? Same as today. But she keeps repeating the words "hands" and "palms" and messing up her lines. It was messing *me* up. Then she says she quits because Shakespeare's a tongue twister.

Me: Well, it is a lot to learn.

Scott: Hey, maybe she *will* quit!

Jayden: *(Storms backstage.)* I heard that! I know what you two are doing back here. For your information, I'm not quitting.

Me: What! We're just talking.

Jayden: *(Fumes.)* I know what you did. You came back here on purpose, just to fog me so Scott and I wouldn't get to—

Scott: Finish our scene?

Me: Jayden, I'm sorry. I guess I hit the button and *poof*! It just went off. I didn't even know it still had fog juice in there.

Jayden: Ha. You are such a little liar.

Scott: Hey, Jayden. It's just a little fog. You don't have to get so bent out of shape about it.

Jayden: Oh, sure, take her side. She's just jealous because for once she didn't get the lead. And now she'll do anything to wreck it.

Me: *(Teases.)* Who? Little Miss Woe Is Me?

Jayden: *(Hits Scott in arm.)* Uh! You told her that? I can't believe you.

Scott: I didn't—are you crazy? I don't know what you're talking about.

Me: *(Shrugs; feigns innocence.)*

Jayden: I'll get you for this, Reel. I'm

going to talk to Mr. Cannon and make sure you're not allowed anywhere near this play.

Me: Good luck. I live here. My parents own this theater.

Jayden: *(Storms off.)*

Me: "Farewell, fair cruelty . . ."

Scott: Hey, I better get going, too. I only have about a thousand lines to memorize by tomorrow. Hey, did you write that sonnet for English?

Me: Yeah, you?

Scott: No sweat. I only have fourteen more lines to go.

Me: But a whole sonnet is only fourteen lines.

Scott: Exactly. That's why I gotta run. See you tomorrow?

Me: I'll be there.

Scott: For what it's worth, I think you woulda made a great Juliet. *(Rushes through curtain and hops down off stage.)*

Me: *(Sticks head through gap in curtain.)* Hey, Romeo. Thanks.

Scott: Hey, Reel. Fog ya later! *(Mimes spraying with fog machine, laughs all the way up the aisle.)*

Boy Meets Soap

It started out as just a perfectly ordinary normal Saturday. Three sisters in the family room, each in her own favorite chair, which we had named years ago. Joey was flopped sideways across the Blue Blob, drawing frog comics in her notebook. Alex was stretched out on Jabba the Couch, moaning about something that happened in English yesterday. Something to do with her sonnet.

I was in my Thinking Chair, waiting for Wire Rims to show up so we could do our science lab and get it over with. I couldn't stop shaking my leg. Nervous? Excited? It was hard for me to tell.

"I'm telling you," said Alex, "it was sooooo embarrassing. We had to make up our own Shakespearean sonnet in English and I got called on to read a love poem in front of the whole world. Now I'm sure Scott knows I like him."

"I don't get it," I said, sitting up. "You like Scott Towel, right? Don't you want him to know?"

"No. It doesn't work that way. Because I don't want him to know I like him before I know for sure that he likes me."

"It's so obvious he likes you," I said.

"It's just like in the *Sealed with a Kiss* movie," said Joey. "See, Romeo likes Juliet, but he tells his friend seal instead of telling her. Meanwhile, Juliet likes Romeo, but she tells another lady seal instead of just telling him. And they think it's all secret and nobody can tell they're in love, but really everybody can."

"Great. My love life is like a cartoon. With stupid seals."

"Since when are you into *Romeo and Juliet*?" I asked Joey. "I thought you hated lovey-dovey stuff."

"I do. But it's okay when they're seals."

Alex sat up and pointed her rolled-up magazine at me. "Hey, whatever happened when that boy called you, Stevie? You never said."

Joey covered her ears, shook her head, and went, "La-la-la-la-la-la-la!" so she wouldn't have to hear.

"What boy? Oh, him. Nothing. Just—we have to do this thing for Science."

"What thing?" Alex asked.

"We have to do a hands-on weather experiment. So we're going to figure out some way to simulate a cloud."

"Oh, yeah, I know some people who did that too. Mr. Petry's class, right? Wait a second. You're going to need water and ice and—you're doing *that* project with a boy?"

"Yeah. He's coming over. So what?"

Joey took her fingers out of her ears. "Here? He's coming here? To our house? Bluck! Why can't you just do it with a normal person, like Olivia?"

"Because Olivia's not even in this class."

"Wait a second," said Alex. "He's coming over here to do the cloud thing? This is big. This is huge. This is—we have to get ready. You know, prepare."

"Prepare for what?"

"First we have to clean the whole house. Then, we work on you. Find you a purple shirt to wear."

"What's wrong with the shirt she has on?" Joey asked.

"Stevie looks good in purple. And we have to fix your hair. And borrow a little blush."

I blushed at the thought of putting on blush.

"It's Science. It's not a date."

"I have an idea," said Joey. "Just wear your pajamas, and *don't* have him over here."

"Stevie, have you even thought about this for two seconds?" Alex asked. "That cloud thing is messy, and you need a lot of water. I'm pretty sure you have to do the cloud thing in the bathtub!"

"So?"

"Bath. Tub," said Alex. "The bath tub is in the bathroom."

"Why? Is it a mess in there?"

"Not that. There's, you know, girl stuff in there."

"Yeah, like my rubber ducky collection," said Joey. "Promise you won't do any science experiments on my rubber duckies. No melting them or anything."

"Girl stuff? Like, are your days-of-the-week undies hanging in there or something?"

"Yeah, or shirts with *words* on them?"

"Joey!" I gave her the evil eye. But Alex wasn't even paying attention.

"I just mean soap and shampoo and toothbrushes and stuff. Do you really want a boy seeing your toothbrush?"

"What's wrong with my toothbrush?" I asked. Maybe I shouldn't have said he could come over. But I sure didn't want to go to his house!

"And . . . there're probably hair balls in the drain," said Joey.

"Eeww," I said.

"Nevermind. Boys love hair balls. Boys *are* hair balls."

"Stop saying 'hair balls,'" I pleaded.

"Hey, I just thought of something. You know why a boy can't see your soap?" Joey joked. "Because boys smell. They don't like soap. They don't even know what soap is. So if a boy comes over, you'd have to be, like, 'Boy. Meet Soap. Soap, this is a boy.'" She laughed herself silly.

"Joey, this is so not helping. I already feel kinda weird as it is," I admitted.

"Kind of weird?" said Joey. "You're weird if you don't know how weird it is."

"Stevie, it'll be fine," said Alex. "Just don't let him near the bathroom."

"But what if he has to, you know, go?"

"Tell him to find a tree," said Joey.

"Joey! I'm not going to—"

"Send him over to the Raven," said Alex.

"Okay, what else? We're going to need a big giant tub of water."

"Ask Dad to blow up the old kiddie pool. And put it in the backyard," Alex suggested. "And don't let him in the family room because it's just so embarrassing with Dad's old props. Like, who has a knight in their living room? And there's zucchini all over the kitchen, so don't let him in there. And promise me you won't wear those pants! And no slippers!"

"What's wrong with my pants?" I had on my favorite jeans with holes in the knees. They looked fine to me. This boy thing sure was complicated.

I made a T with my hands. "Time out, time out, you guys. Alex, I'm not wearing makeup or anything! It's not like I *like* him, like him. He's just a friend. If that. I barely know him. So I'm just going to be myself. And Joey? Boys aren't that bad. They don't all smell and burp and punch you and stuff. So just think of him like Olivia. Only with glasses."

Alex looked down at her hands. Joey stared at the carpet. Neither sister said a word for close to three minutes.

"I'm just saying. If he has to come over, stay outside and don't let him inside the house," Joey said.

"What's wrong with him coming in the house?"

Joey hit her hand to her head in exasperation. "One. I'm here. Two. Boy cooties!"

Froggy Soap Opera
by Joey Reel
Fred Frog is coming over. Do I look too green?
You're a frog!
What if I have fly breath?
I thought you were JUST FRIENDS.
NO BOY FROGS ALLOWED
What if he sees my Froggy Bubble Bath?
What a SOAP opera!

Ker-Plunk!

I was already waiting for him in the backyard when Wire Rims showed up. With muffins. And a party bag of ice. He was wearing a faded T-shirt that said TRAILER PARK SANTAS.

Between bites of muffins, Wire Rims and I stood under an overcast sky, staring at the orange clown fish and pink starfish on the bottom of Joey's old kiddie pool. The morning fog had never burned off, making the edges of things fuzzy. Kind of how I imagined it would be if you wore glasses but you were looking at the world without them.

Every time I glanced back at the house, I saw Mom looking out the kitchen window. At us. Embarrassing!

"Okay. Here's the plan," I said, trying not to think about Mom checking up on us. "When I throw in the last bucket of hot water, you get the camera ready to take a picture. Then I'll quick grab the black towel and hold it up in the background, so our cloud will show up really good."

Wire Rims raised his eyebrows at me over his glasses.

"Was I being too bossy?" I asked. "Sorry. I'm just saying."

"Okay. On the count of three. Ready?" said Wire Rims. "One, two, three." I leaned over and poured the bucket of hot water into the pool. Then I grabbed the towel and held it high. *Click. Click. Click. Click. Click.* Wire Rims snapped a bunch of pictures.

I let the towel drop. "Did you see what I saw? That was *so* not a cloud. That was barely a puff."

"I just took five shots of a big fat nothing," said Wire Rims. "I've had bigger clouds on my glasses when they steam up."

"Okay, genius, what'd we do wrong?" I teased.

"I did this with some kids at my old school and it worked. Honest!"

Mom poked her head out the back door. "Stevie? Do you need more hot water? Or I can put the kettle on, if you think—"

"Just a second, Mom," I called, hoping to brush her off. She went back into the house.

I flipped through my notebook, looking over my notes. "So. We know a cloud forms when rising air cools to the point where some of the molecules clump together."

"We do?" he asked.

I couldn't tell if he was teasing, but I thought so. "Yes. We do. But only if we were paying attention in class. C'mon, you know, like all that stuff about how warm air rises from the surface and meets colder air?"

"If you say so," said Wire Rims, grinning at me.

"Get serious," I said, reaching out to punch him on the arm. I took my hand back.

"Get *cirrus*?" Wire Rims joked.

"I get it. Cloud joke. Nice. Very funny." I chewed on the end of my pencil. "So, if the water's warm, and we poured in a bunch of ice, it should have worked, right?"

"Yeah. We poured in two buckets of hot water and one whole bag of ice," said Wire Rims. "Party size."

"Maybe the water has to be hotter," I said. "We should boil water this time, before we throw it in."

"And more ice," said Wire Rims. "Do you have more ice? I think I remember last time we used way more ice to go for, you know, the contrast. It's all about the contrast."

"Very scientific." I smiled at Wire Rims.

"You know what I mean," he said, looking down and fiddling with the buttons on his camera.

"Sure," I said, staring at a lone ice cube bobbing on the surface.

"How's it going?" Mom asked, the back door slamming behind her. This time, she came out holding two different plates of strange-looking lumps.

"What are those?" I asked. "They look weird."

"Cookies," said Mom.

"I'll try one," said Wire Rims, picking up a lump from the red plate and taking a big bite.

"I'm experimenting with ways to use tofu in recipes for kids, but, you know, hide it so they don't know they're eating protein."

Wire Rims was eating his cookie and smacking his lips like he had peanut butter stuck to the roof of his mouth.

"So, what do you think?" Mom asked.

"Um, I'll try one of these," he said, brushing crumbs off his shirt and taking a cookie from the other plate.

"Mom, please? We have to get back to our experiment before the water gets too cooled off."

"You won't try one, Stevie? I'd love your opinion."

"Mom. Can we do this later?"

"Okay, okay. But something's missing. I have to figure out what." Mom was shaking her head.

"Vanilla," I said. "Now, we have to get back to our Science thing." Mom carried the cookie plates back into the house. "You didn't have to eat them, you know," I told Wire Rims. "How bad was it?"

"No, um, they were, um, fine."

"Seriously?"

"Okay, okay," he said, glancing back at the house. "They taste like papier-mâché!" I threw back my head, cracking up.

"That was really nice of you not to spit them out. Trust me. She's going to come back with more. Just tell her you're full. You had a big lunch."

"Full. Got it. Thanks."

I sat down on the edge of the inflated pool. "So. Are you sure you didn't get any pictures?" I asked Wire Rims.

He sat down next to me and started clicking through the pictures. "Black towel. Black towel. Black towel. Black towel. Your elbow," he said.

"Aw, frog," I said. "What if it doesn't work and we can't get a picture?"

"Frog, huh?"

"I guess my little sister, Joey, is starting to rub off on me. She's way into frogs. She found one after that big storm we had, and she adopted it and named it Sir Croaks-a-Lot."

"Sir Croaks-a-Lot, huh? That would make a cool name for a band."

"Like Don't Poke the Yeti?"

"D'you know them? They played at a coffeehouse and my older brother took me. It was slammin'."

"Slammin'? We better start *slammin'* on our Science project."

Mom poked her head out the door. Again. "Kids? I'm walking down to the market to get some vanilla. Need anything?"

"No thanks, Mom," I said impatiently.

"Okay, I'll be back in twenty minutes. If you need anything, ask Dad. He's right next door at the Raven."

"Bye, Mom," I said. Wire Rims gave an awkward wave.

"Wait a second." I grabbed his arm to get his attention. "Sorry. I was just thinking . . . If we can't get this to work, my dad has a fog machine, right at the theater next door. Maybe we could use it to make a cloud."

"Whoa, hold on there, Freaky Friday. What happened to Stevie? Because if your idea is to fake a cloud with the fogger? I think they call that cheating," he teased.

"Well, I mean, that's only if we're, you know, super desperate. Like, we used all the hot water in the whole entire house and all the ice from the ice machine at the gas station down the street."

"Or . . . I could just Photoshop a cloud into the picture on the computer."

"Aha! So what you're saying is, you're a bigger cheater pants than me. At least with the fogger, we're doing something to simulate a cloud."

We both cracked up. I caught myself laughing and couldn't help thinking how much fun I was having. But we still had to figure out the cloud thing. I looked up at a passing cloud in the sky. Big mistake.

That's when it happened.

Before you could say *cumulonimbus,* everything started to spin. Wire Rims's bug eyes were in my face, and his glasses poked me in the forehead. His marshmallow nose smushed up against mine.

And just like that, smack, he *KISSED ME*!

Instantly, I jerked my head back to get away from the kiss. My arms windmilled as I tried to get my balance.

But it was too late.

Ker-plunk! I toppled backward into the kiddie pool, making a whale of a splash. We're talking a tidal wave. No, a tsunami!

Wire Rims jumped back. "Ahh!" I yelled as the icy water slid down my back. I felt strangely hot and cold at the same time.

When I sat up, I was dripping wet. My hoodie filled with water, a mop of hair hung down over my eyes, and bubbles burbled from the hole in my jeans.

"Omigod, Stevie, I'm so—I mean, I'm sorry—here—let me—" Wire Rims reached out a hand to help me up, but I didn't take it.

"Leave me alone!" I practically shouted. Mortified, I hauled myself up out of the pool, yanked the towel from his hands, snapped it around my shoulders, and ran for the house.

I stayed in the shower for a way long time, letting the hot water stream down my face.

I felt like the rain.

I closed my eyes until there was nothing but me and the warm water. Not because I was cold, but because I had to be alone.

I wiped the steam from the window in our shower and stared out at the dark clouds over the mountains. Fifteen minutes ago there had actually been patches of blue sky. Puffy clouds like snowy cauliflower. Now low, dark, ragged clouds blocked out the sunlight, warning of more bad weather. How could clouds change shape that quickly?

A jet stream of emotions went through me—scared, angry, confused.

I closed my eyes. Om . . . One, two, three, four . . . Humpty Dumpty sat on a wall . . . Hail Mary Full of Grace . . .

Thump. Thump. I could hear my own heart pounding. No, somebody was pounding on the bathroom door. "Somebody's in here," I yelled over the beat of the water.

"Stevie? Are you okay? You've been in there forever." *Joey.*

I turned off the water and hugged myself into a thick, cozy towel, wrapping it around me. The mirror was so steamy I couldn't see myself. *Oh, so now a cloud forms,* I couldn't help thinking.

I cut a swath through the steam on the mirror with the side of my fist, not sure who I'd find looking back at me.

"Stevie?" *Joey again.*

It was me. Still Stevie.

I peered at my reflection. I guess I'd been worried I might not recognize myself, but the face in the mirror *looked* like the same me.

Finally, I cracked open the door, stuck my head out. "Joey. Is anybody here?"

"Just me. The boy left. Alex is next door at the theater with Dad."

"Go get Alex. Tell her we have to have an emergency Sisters Club meeting."

"Now?" Joey asked.

"Don't let her say no."

Boy Cooties!

I huddled in the corner of my bed against the wall, wrapped in my fuzzy mint-green robe, hugging a pillow to me and waiting for my sisters. What was taking them so long? I pulled out my Science notebook and started scribbling, trying to make sense of my confusion.

Ask a question: Why did Wire Rims try to kiss me?
Form a hypothesis (Your best guess): Because I asked him over? Because I grabbed his arm? Because he *likes me* likes me?
Gather materials: No kiddie pools!
Conduct experiment: Once was more than enough!
Observations: To avoid boy cooties, keep your

eyes on your science experiment. Boys and kiddie pools do not play well together. Boys who eat papier-mâché cookies to be nice are not to be trusted. Kisses can throw you off balance.

Interpret data: He wanted to see me fall in the pool and get soaking wet? Scuba equipment necessary when conducting science experiments. Tofu cookies make you psycho!

Draw conclusions: I thought we were friends. I even wondered if I just-maybe-might like him. But I am so not ready for this!

"What's the big emergency?" Alex said in an irritated voice, standing in the doorway and crossing her arms in front of her. "What happened to your friend? And what are you doing up here in your bathrobe in the middle of the day? Why are you all wet?"

"Please don't get all crossy-armsy on me. I had to call an emergency sisters meeting because I really needed to talk."

She softened a little, uncrossing her arms and coming into the room. Joey sat cross-legged on the floor, staring up at me.

At first, my tongue felt about as thick as a dictionary. I couldn't find words. Maybe I was afraid that once I started talking, I'd tell too much.

"Stevie? What is it?" Alex sat down on the bed next to me. "You have three minutes. Dad's waiting for me to test the balcony. Can't you talk to Mom or something?"

"No!" I said a little too forcefully. Then the words started gushing out of me. "It was terrible. Horrible. So totally embarrassing! One minute we were just joking around and everything was perfectly normal, and then I fell in a pool of ice water like a dripping-wet octopus . . . my arms everywhere . . . and so freezing and all of a sudden . . . I got kissed! At least I think I did."

Joey gaped at me like I was speaking Alien. Even her stuffed chipmunk wouldn't stop giving me a glassy-eyed stare. "Oh, no, not you, too. I can't take all this boy stuff!" Joey moaned.

"What!" Alex said, enunciating the *T* like she was spitting at me. She jumped to her feet like she'd been stung. "You fell in the pool and you were sopping wet and that boy kissed you? I can't believe it."

"What? That a boy kissed me?"

"No. That my little sister got her first kiss before me! This is great. Just great. Welcome to my Ugly Betty life." She crossed her arms again.

"I can't believe you're mad. This isn't about you. It's, like, the worst thing ever, and it happened to me. *Me,*" I said, stabbing myself in the chest with my finger.

"So? I'm the one who wanted a first kiss. You could care less. And I'm, like, the star of *Never Been Kissed.*"

"I can't believe a boy kissed you. *Ew!*" Joey shuddered like she had creepy crawlies on her. "I'd rather touch a big fat banana slug. No, I'd rather eat a worm!"

"You guys, I'm telling you—I've never been so embarrassed in my whole life! I mean, how would you feel if you acted like a total idiot, fell backward into your Science experiment, turned into a human Popsicle, then said something mean and ran away?"

"This is bad," said Joey. "Bad." She was shaking her head.

"Thanks a lot, Joey," I said.

"Are you *sure* he kissed you?" Alex asked. "How exactly did you fall into the pool? Walk us through it," she said, rolling her hand in circles to get me to tell the story.

"Hold on," said Joey. She ran into Alex's room and came back with Sock Monkey. "Here. Sock Monkey can be Wire Rims." She grabbed a pair of wire-rimmed glasses off of her doll with the long braids and put them on Sock Monkey.

"Hey, he actually looks cute with glasses!" said Alex. I scowled at her. "Okay, that is *so* not the point." She handed him to me.

I told the whole story, in all its horribleness, complete with putting Sock Monkey in my face to demonstrate the glasses hitting me in the head. Then I showed them how I pulled away, leaning backward, flailing my arms and losing my balance.

"Only pretend the bed is the pool of water and pretend I'm soaking wet. Watch. I'll show you." I demonstrated falling back on the bed dramatically and almost hit my head on the wall.

Both of my sisters started laughing like idiots.

"I hate you guys. This is so not funny!"

"You know you can't sleep in our room tonight," said Joey. "You have *major* boy cooties."

"Stevie, so what if you got wet? You still got your first kiss! You are so lucky. I hate my life!"

"Why can't everything go back to the way it was?" Joey asked sulkily.

"So, then what happened?" Alex pressed.

"I ran."

"Did he say anything?"

"He was . . . stuttering. I don't know."

"Did you say anything?"

"I don't think so. I might have yelled at him."

"Oh, man, that is, like, the worst first kiss ever!" said Alex.

I clobbered Alex with the pillow I was holding. "It's all your fault, Alex."

"Me? What'd I do?"

"You made us throw stuff in the fire that night. You made us wish stuff. I tossed in my troll doll and wished for something new and exciting to happen to me. Instead, I got first-kissed by a troll in a Santa shirt."

"At least your hair didn't turn green," said Alex.

"That would be cooler," said Joey.

"I want the spell off me," I said with a shiver. "Is

there, like, a double-reverse, *anti*–first kiss spell or something?"

"Yeah, right," said Alex. "Uh! My baby sister got kissed first."

"Gross me out," said Joey.

"I just can't believe this happened to me," said Alex.

"To you? You guys! How about . . . I can never show my face at school again. At least not in Earth Science or in the halls or at lunch. And I'll just have to flunk my Science lab. Forget it. I'm never leaving this house again." I leaned back and put the pillow over my head. "That's it. From now on, I'm going to wear this pillow case over my head when I go to school."

"Can I take your picture?" Joey asked.

Ten Reasons Not to Kiss a Boy
by Joey Reel

1. Boy cooties.
2. Breath as bad as an elephant seal's.
3. Slobber factor: 11 on a scale of 1 to 10.
4. Nose-smushing factor: 9 on a scale of 1 to 10.
5. Cross-eyed factor: 7 on a scale of 1 to 10.
6. Think about it: Those same lips have probably eaten a worm (or dirt) at some point.
7. Ancient Egyptians (and seals) kiss by rubbing noses; boys don't.
8. I'd rather kiss a frog.
9. They might kiss you back.
10. The next day they'll punch you.

Animals Don't Kiss
by Joey Reel, Animal Lover

How did the boy make the girl fall in the swimming pool?
He kissed her! Ha, ha, ha, ha, ha, ha!

Sick! Stevie got kissed! By a real, live, cootified boy. Yuck! That's like a 10 on the Grossometer.

If you ask me, animals got it right. Animals don't kiss (except maybe chimps, some apes, and rainbow lorikeets). I saw it on Animal Planet.

- Dolphins and whales touch noses.
  Gross factor: 2
- Dogs, wolves, and foxes lick faces.
  Gross factor: 7
- Tigers rub faces and whiskers. Cute!
  Gross factor: 0
- Kissing fish are really fighting. Cool!
  Gross factor: 2

- Birds tap beaks. (Throwing up food for each other!)
  Gross factor: 9
- Snails touch antennae.
  Gross factor: 4
- Elephants put trunks in mouth. Ouch!
  Gross factor: 8
- Bonobo apes kiss. (Hey, they're apes!)
  Gross factor: 10

TO BE OR NOT TO BE . . . TYBALT
Starring Alex

Me: Sock Monkey! You're never going to believe what I just heard.

Sock Monkey: Don't you mean *over*heard?

Me: Busted. I admit it. I was listening in on play practice again. I can't help it— I miss being part of the play.

Sock Monkey: So, tell me!

Me: Okay, so Tybalt, a.k.a. some kid named Conrad Icches, just threw in the towel. As in *quit the play.* As in *walked out the door*!

Sock Monkey: Who's Tybalt?

Me: Tybalt is Juliet's cousin, and a Capulet. He hates all Montagues, especially Romeo. He's the one, at the ball, who realizes it's Romeo in disguise and wants to kill him on the spot. Except he can't because Lord Capulet would get super mad. So later, he sends a letter to Romeo and challenges him to a big duel, where they'll fight to the death. So cool! I was made for this part.

Sock Monkey: What? I thought you were made for the part of Juliet. Besides, you quit, remember?

Me: I know, but I made a mistake, okay? I never really wanted to quit. I think I just freaked when I couldn't be Juliet. But every day when I hear them practice—I don't know, it's like I'm missing out. Like something's wrong. A piece of me is missing when I'm not acting in a play.

Sock Monkey: But you can't be Tybalt. Tybalt hates Romeo. You like Romeo.

Me: So? He has, like, the best part, even though he hardly has any speaking lines, because he gets to sword-fight all the time. They call him the Prince of Cats because he's so great at sword-fighting. He can even kill a mouse, no problem.

Sock Monkey: But he's a boy, right?

Me: Yeah, but the boys get to do all the cool action stuff. The girl characters just fold their hands and swoon and faint all the time. It's boring just waving a handkerchief around.

Sock Monkey: So, you would dress up as a boy, even though Jayden is the lead. And she'll be in a silky, satiny, frilly dress?

Me: For one thing, I already have the short hair. Besides, at least this way I get to be in the play. I can't spend my whole life eavesdropping on them.

Sock Monkey: You mean, at least you'd get to be around Scott Towel, because you'd have scenes with him.

Me: That too.

Sock Monkey: And you guys would have to practice together *a lot,* like as much as with Jayden, because the sword-fighting scenes are really hard.

Me: Exactly. Wouldn't you just love to see the look on Jayden's face when she finds out I'm in the play? She's still a measle-mouthed maggot. A moldwarp. A beslubbering flax-wench!

Sock Monkey: Tell us how you *really* feel.

Me: It would just kill her if I got a good part in the play.

Sock Monkey: To be or *not* to be Tybalt. That is the question.

Me: I think I'm really going to do it. Yep. Now, all I have to do is convince Mr. Cannon that he should give me another chance. Even though I quit.

Sock Monkey: How are you going to do that?

Me: Hey, I grew up sword-fighting my sisters using paper towel tubes. Dad taught us tons of stuff. Who could possibly know the thrust, the lunge, the high-low sequence, and going for the kill better than me?

Sock Monkey: Sounds like you're the man for the job!

True or False
by Joey Reel

PU!

True or false? Take the quiz:

- Boys have 10,000 more sweat glands than girls do.
  Totally TRUE!

- The science of kissing is called grossology.
  FALSE. It's called philematology. Do not study this!

- A one-minute kiss burns 260 calories.
  FALSE. It only burns 26 calories.
  Play a sport instead!

- In Roman times, a kiss on the cheek was called an osculum.
  TRUE. My advice: Stay away from Rome.

- In Ancient Egypt, a kiss on the nose was called a sneezer.
  FALSE. I made that up. But they did kiss with their noses.

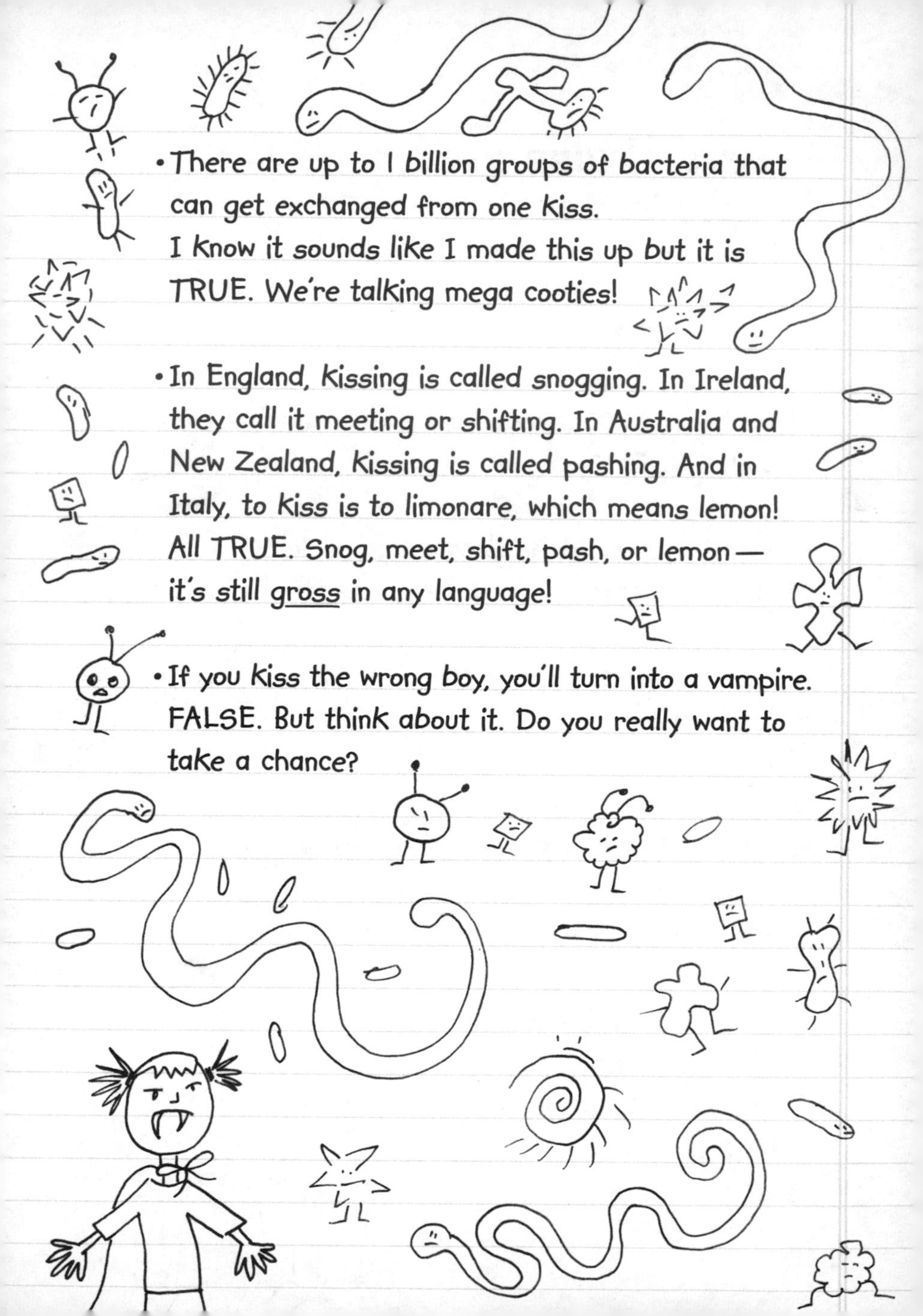

• There are up to 1 billion groups of bacteria that can get exchanged from one kiss.
I know it sounds like I made this up but it is TRUE. We're talking mega cooties!

• In England, kissing is called snogging. In Ireland, they call it meeting or shifting. In Australia and New Zealand, kissing is called pashing. And in Italy, to kiss is to limonare, which means lemon! All TRUE. Snog, meet, shift, pash, or lemon — it's still gross in any language!

• If you kiss the wrong boy, you'll turn into a vampire. FALSE. But think about it. Do you really want to take a chance?

FRENCH-FRIED FRENEMIES

Starring Alex

SETTING: THE RAVEN THEATER; PLAY PRACTICE, THE NEXT AFTERNOON.

Jayden: What's she doing here?

Scott: Um, she lives here?

Mr. Cannon: Everyone, I'd like you to welcome our newest addition to *Romeo and Juliet*—Alex Reel.

Matt: Hey, Alex.

Brianna: Alex is back?

Allen/Alvin: We need you . . . we really need you.

Jayden: Mr. Cannon, I thought Brianna was going to be my understudy.

Me: Hi, everybody. I'm happy to be back! I was, um, super busy and thought I might not have time for the play, you know? But then I heard about Conrad quitting and got the idea that maybe I could help out and fill in for him. So, I talked it over with Mr. Cannon, and he said yes.

Mr. Cannon: We're very pleased to have you back, Alex.

Jayden: I don't get it. Conrad was Tybalt. Juliet's cousin. Hello! He's a *guy.*

Me: That's me. Tybalt. *(Tugs on short hair and holds finger under nose, imitating a mustache.)*

Mr. Cannon: Alex has been good enough to step up and take Conrad's place and play the role of Tybalt. That saves us from holding auditions again, since we're already behind.

Jayden: *(To Alex.) You're* going to be Tybalt?

Scott: *(To Alex.)* You're going to be *Tybalt*?

Mr. Cannon: I, for one, think it's a great idea. Mix it up a little. In Shakespeare's time, all the actors were men, and they had to play female parts.

Me: So, this is like that, only in reverse.

Mr. Cannon: I couldn't be more pleased. This will be a good challenge for you,

Alex. And the rest of us can learn a thing or two from Alex. Alex is quite the accomplished swordswoman. Or should I say swords*man.*

Jayden: *(Looks pleased. Turns to Scott.)* Romeo *kills* Tybalt, you know. So, you're going to have to kill her.

Scott: *(Turns to Alex.)* Wait . . . I have to kill you? Oh, yeah, after you kill Mercutio, I kill you.

Me: Don't worry. I'm good at dying.

Mr. Cannon: Okay, people. Let's have Romeo and Juliet, stage left, starting with "I would I were thy bird." Alex, why don't you work with Mercutio while they finish up. Then you and Romeo can practice some swashbuckling.

LATER THAT AFTERNOON, SWORD-FIGHTING LESSON WITH ROMEO.

Me: Okay, we'll start out using these wrapping-paper tubes for swords. *(Hands him a long cardboard tube.)*

Scott: Can't we just start out with French fries? *(Grabs French fry from grease-stained white bag and waves it at Alex.)* On guard!

Me: Okay, you are seriously weird. *(Takes bite.)* Yum! Okay, no more fries for you. Here's your cardboard tube.

Scott: Yeah, because I wouldn't want to hurt you. I swashbuckle a mean sword, you know.

Me: Very funny. Okay, first, we take position. Stand facing me with your feet wide apart and bend your knees.

Scott: Like this?

Me: Yes, except don't bend your knees so much. You look like a first grader with a stomachache.

Scott: Is this where I get to kill you?

Me: *(Laughs.)* Not if I kill you first.

Scott: So what are we, like, frenemies?

Me: *(Hands on hips.)* Pay attention! Okay, now stand back a little. The tip of your sword should be about twelve inches from my belly button. Hold the sword in your right hand and point it to your left, at my side, right about here, at my waist. Never point the sword directly *at* the other person.

Scott: How can I kill you if I can't point the sword at you?

Me: *(Teases.)* For now, I'll just be happy if you don't poke my eyes out.

Scott: Yeah, those are great eyes. To have, I mean. I'm sure you want to keep them both.

Me: Okay, now watch me first. Raise your right arm, move it clockwise up and over your head, and our swords meet in the middle. Try it.

Scott: Like this?

Me: Great! When the tips of our swords are touching, it's called the top hat position. Now, lower your right arm to your left again and bring the swords together again at our feet.

Scott: How about this?

Me: Okay, but try not to take my arm off, either.

Scott: Sorry.

Me: Try again. By yourself this time. I'll be . . . stage left. As in far away.

Scott: Ha, ha. Seriously, I can do this. I promise not to poke your green eyes out.

Me: Maybe I should wear protective headgear. Like, a face helmet?

Scott: *(Glides tube through air, over head, and down to feet.)*

Me: That was great. Perfect. Now, we both go at the same time. Top hat position first, then down to our feet. Think of it like a dance.

Scott: Whoa, whoa, wait a second here. You had to say "dance"? Forget it. I'm a horrible dancer.

Me: No way. You danced in *Hairspray*, and you were fine.

Scott: You remember that? We were, like, seven. All I had to do, pretty much, was stand on some lady's feet and she twirled me around.

Me: Well, don't think your big clown feet are coming anywhere near my toes. C'mon. It just takes practice. Try.

Scott: *(Raises sword to top hat position, back down to feet.)*

Me: Perfect! See? Was that so bad?

Scott: You're a good teacher.

Me: Thanks. Now we're going to start downstage and move upstage. Just remember, keep a safe distance from me, and never let your sword cross the other person's face. Your moves should be *around* me, not at me. Pretend you have an invisible force field around you.

Scott: So, I'm like Superman or Green Lantern or something?

Me: *(Laughs.)* You know what I mean.

Scott: Okay, no, seriously, I think I got it. Wow. That wasn't bad. I have to say I was really dreading this part.

Me: One more thing. Tomorrow we add footwork.

Scott: Footwork? *(Slaps head.)* Aw, you mean dancing! Are you sure I can't just stand on your feet or something?

Me: Yeah, right. We're mortal enemies. You hate me.

Scott: That's gonna be hard, but I'll try to remember. *(Looks at floor.)*

Me: Then I'll teach you the lunge, then we'll add the kill to the high-low sequence.

Scott: Is that a promise?

Me: Okay, you ready?

Scott: Ready. *(Clunking of paper tubes ensues.)*

Me: Good! That's good!

Scott: *(Holds his side in pain.)* Oh, no!

Me: What?

Scott: Um, I hate to say anything, but you just stabbed me in the force field.

Me: Romeo, thou art a villain.

Cheese Crackers and Cheese Weasels

Monday. I dreaded the day I would have to go back to school and face Wire Rims, but it came anyway, just as I predicted. Whoever invented Mondays should get sent to permanent detention.

When I got to school, I didn't see any sign of Wire Rims in the halls. Phew. I was safe until Earth Science.

I made it through morning recess. Still no sign of Wire Rims. But then it was time for Earth Science, and I knew I couldn't put it off any longer.

"What am I going to do?" I asked Olivia, biting and ripping half the nail off my finger. "I mean, I freaked and just left him there. Just thinking of having to talk to him makes me want to throw up."

"Well, you *have* to talk to him."

"Easy for you to say."

"Look. I don't see why you can't just like him. I mean, it's obvious he likes you. And you do like him, right?"

"How many times do I have to tell you? Not like that."

"Well, I like him."

"Then *you* kiss him."

"Gross. I don't like him that way."

"Hello! Me either!"

"So, tell him you hate his guts. Tell him not to come near you again."

"It's not like that."

"Stevie, you're driving me bonkers, you know that?"

I tried to tell myself it was going to be fine. But my stomach felt like I'd just stepped off the Tilt-A-Whirl.

Be strong, I willed myself. *You can do this. You recited a poem in front of the entire Language Arts class. You sang in front of 457 people* on stage. *You entered a cupcake contest that was almost all grown-ups.*

When I got to Earth Science, I couldn't help looking directly at the second-to-last chair in the fourth row. Empty. He wasn't even here!

I took my seat in the back. Maybe I'd been all

worried for nothing. Maybe he hadn't even come to school today. I felt my stomach unclench. I could breathe again.

"Are you looking for that kid Owen?" said the girl next to me.

"Yeah, um, we're partners for the weather experiment thingie we're doing."

"It's weird—I knew he was in this class, but I saw him just now heading into the auditorium."

"The auditorium? But . . . that's where it flooded. It's all closed down. Nobody's supposed to go in there for, like, a month."

"Maybe he's signing up for Drama Club." She shrugged.

"Now? He's already late. Mr. Petry's going to give him det—"

That's when it hit me. Wire Rims was cutting class! *He* was avoiding me, not the other way around. He must hate my guts for freaking out and running away like that. I was mean to him. What if he never wanted to talk to me again?

I could hardly concentrate all morning. In Earth Science, I made up some lame excuse about why I didn't have our Weather Lab project. And in Language

Arts, Ms. Carter-Dunne passed back our persuasive essays. It reminded me of that first day with Wire Rims, when I had to spend detention with him in this very room. It seemed like months ago.

My mind wandered. I glanced back at the magnetic poetry board behind me. Tons of new similes were spelled out all over the board.

Gossamer as grasshopper wing
Sad as he-loves-me-not daisy
Groovy as moon in June

What was it he'd called me that day with the Seventies magnets? *Cellular? Stellular!*

At the very bottom of the board, two words caught my eye. *Hey Sunshine.* Just like that day we'd spelled out silly messages to each other. Was this some kind of secret message Wire Rims had left for me? Wanted me to see? Or just a coincidence?

Hey Sunshine
Dark Cloud over me
Sorry I M a Cheese Weasel

Maybe Wire Rims wasn't so mad after all. Suddenly, I couldn't wait for class to be over.

As soon as the bell rang, I headed out the door—not to lunch, where I was supposed to be, but all the way to the other end of the building. I ducked under the yellow CAUTION tape and pulled open the door of the auditorium.

The carpet had been ripped up and peeled back in places, and giant fans hummed, working to dry out the whole place. The lights were off, and it was spooky dark except for a crack of light leaking out from beneath the curtain on stage. I raced down the aisle, leapfrogging over heaps of old carpet, and climbed up the stairs to the stage, searching for the opening in the big velvet curtain.

There he was, all alone, hunched against the back wall, dwarfed by towers of upside-down chairs, scaffolding, a broken-down castle from *Once Upon a Mattress,* and a scarred piano. He had earphones on and was scribbling in a spiral notebook in his lap. An old-fashioned desk lamp plugged in beside him cast a small halo of light.

"Hey," I said softly. I was so nervous it came out like a mouse squeak.

He looked up, and for the first time, I noticed his deep gray eyes, not his glasses.

"Oh. Hey." He pulled out one ear bud. Then he looked down again, tapping the end of his pencil on his notebook. "Did you know that out of four hundred and fifty-six Bob Dylan songs, the word 'cloud' shows up a total of twenty-three times? 'Wind' shows up in fifty-five of them. 'Rain' is in forty of his songs, and 'sky' appears a whopping thirty-six times."

"I did not know that," I said.

"Hurricane, lightning, thunder, and flood are in there a lot too. But I haven't counted those yet."

He ran out of stuff to say. I just stood there, afraid to speak in case my voice came out all shaky again.

"It's very scientific," he went on, trying to fill the awkward pause. "I'm making a graph. You know, for my Earth Science report. But I already told you that, didn't I?"

Finally, I went over and slid my back down the wall next to him, chin on my knees. "So, I had to come find you. I was worried that maybe you had tofu cookie poisoning or something."

Wire Rims let out a laugh. "Nothing like that."

"So, you're just going to hide out here, huh? Backstage? Until they come to remodel the auditorium and somebody finds you back here all cobwebby and covered in dust bunnies and your face looks all bony like that skeleton from *Psycho* . . ." I sucked in my cheeks to show him how he'd look as a psycho skeleton from not eating for, like, a year.

"I have three peanut butter crackers." He held up a half-eaten package of bright orange crackers. "Sorry, I ate the Fruit Roll-Up."

"Forget starvation. The artificial coloring or the salmonella will kill you first."

"You're seriously weird, you know that?"

"I know. You know what else I am? Starving. I'm missing lunch right now." I was hoping he'd want to go to lunch, and everything could go back to being normal.

Instead, he offered me a cracker. "Death cracker?"

I shook my head. "Thanks anyway." For the next few minutes, the only sound was Wire Rims munching on crackers. I couldn't tell if he was still mad.

"So, how long were you planning on hiding out back here?" I asked.

"At least the rest of the day. Maybe the rest of the week. Depends on Bill and Harry."

"Who are Bill and Harry?"

"Work guys. They haven't busted me yet."

I zipped and unzipped the pocket of my backpack. Nervous habit. "You can't just keep cutting Earth Science, you know—you'll end up right smack back in detention."

"Detention's all right. Detention is for cheese weasels. And I'm, like, the world's biggest cheese weasel."

"You're not a cheese weasel. I freaked, okay? It's me, not you. Don't be mad. I'm sorry. I'm so embarrassed." I put my head down on my knees. I wasn't sure what else to say. All I could do was be myself. *To thine own self be true.*

I stared a hole in the floor in front of me. I couldn't look at him. "But, I guess, I mean, I like you, Owen." My face turned twenty shades of red. "Can't we just be friends? Without any weirdness?"

He looked across at me and grinned.

"What?" I couldn't help smiling. "What's so funny?"

"Nothing."

"Ya-huh. You're grinning like the Grinch when he stole Christmas."

"Is that a simile or a metaphor?" he teased.

"I don't know. I don't care! Just tell me what I did." I picked up his notebook and swatted him with it. "C'mon. Tell me what's so funny."

"Nothing, it's just, um, you called me Owen."

An apple a day . . .

WHO IS THE APPLE OF YOUR EYE?

1. Find an apple with a stem.
2. Hold the stem in one hand.
3. Now twist the apple around and around with the other. While you twist, say the letters of the alphabet out loud. A-B-C-D-E, etc.

4. When the stem breaks, stop!

What letter were you on? Now you know the first initial of the One You Love! Was it S for Sock Monkey?

WHO WILL YOU MARRY?

1. Stick an apple seed to your forehead. (Don't worry if you feel silly.)
2. Start to say the alphabet. When the apple seed falls off, stop! What letter were you on?

Guess what? Now you know the first initial of the person you will marry! *Hint: Stand in front of a mirror so you can see when the seed falls off.*

LET THE APPLE BE YOUR CRYSTAL BALL!

What does YOUR future hold?

1. Cut an apple in half.
2. Count the number of seeds you find inside.

- An even number means that you will have good luck in your future.
- An odd number means that bad luck may be headed your way.
- What?! You found a seed cut in half? That can only mean ONE THING. Your future is uncertain.

MUSTACHE AND ALL
Starring Alex

Me: *(Backstage, dressed as Tybalt.)*

Scott: *(Dressed as Romeo; paces and mouths Shakespeare; rapidly twirls and untwirls cord from his shirt.)*

Me: Hey, you. How do I look?

Scott: Like I want to kill you!

Me: Ha, ha. Funny. So, dress rehearsal? Can you believe it?

Scott: Oh, I can believe it. I've been dreading this night for a long time.

Me: What? *(Touches him on arm.)* Stop pacing and look at me for one second. I've never seen you this nervous. What's wrong?

Scott: Forget it. It's nothing. It's just . . . hard to talk about.

Me: Hey, it's me. We've been through dress rehearsals tons of times. Are you worried about your lines? Afraid you'll screw up the sword fighting? I know you're going to do great. We've practiced it, like, a hundred times.

Scott: I wish. Nope. It's not the sword fighting. *That* I have down.

Me: What, then? If you tell me, maybe I can help.

Scott: Um, no, you're, like, the last person who can help.

Me: *(Frustrated.)* Fine.

Scott: Hey, I didn't mean it like that. It's just . . . well . . . Jayden.

Me: Oh, no. What about Jayden?

Scott: *(Shakes head.)* This is so embarrassing!

Me: What?

Scott: I have to kiss her!

Me: *(Pauses, takes deep breath.)* So? You guys have practiced this, right?

Scott: *No!* That's just it! Every time we rehearsed the scene, something happened, you know, to interrupt us. Like, she got fogged! And Mr. Cannon never got back to it.

Me: But tonight's the real thing. You have to go through the whole play just like it'll be on opening night.

Scott: So, I was wondering . . . do you think you could maybe, like, be standing by with the fog machine again?

Me: Um, I think once was enough on the fogging thing.

Scott: Too bad. I gotta think of something!

Me: Scott. You're an actor. You're Romeo. Romeo has to kiss Juliet. Or there wouldn't be a play. The show must go on, and all that junk. *(Wait! What am I saying?)*

Scott: Do you think Romeo could kiss her on the hand?

Me: Sorry. No. C'mon, she's not *that* bad.

Scott: Oh, yeah? If you don't mind swapping spit with a Flutternutter.

Me: *Fluffer*nutter. Marshmallow stuff? Like you put on a sandwich when you're a kid? Never mind. *(Holds out pretend sword.)* En garde!

Scott: *(Laughs.)* C'mon, be serious? You gotta help me.

Me: How?

Scott: Like, give me some stage directions or some ideas on how to get through this.

Me: I'm not going to *help* you kiss Jayden Pffeffer!

Scott: You mean *Juliet.*

Me: Fine.

Scott: Okay, so what should I do? If I want it to look real and everything, I mean.

Me: Okay, first, don't think about Jayden. *(Think about me!)*

Scott: Done.

Me: Just think about Juliet, and how Romeo would feel, and try to be in the moment, ya know?

Scott: Okay . . .

Me: Then, um, well, let's see. If it was me, and I was hoping for the perfect kiss, you know? I'd say, pretend kind of like you're slow dancing . . .

Scott: Okay, you lost me there. You know I don't dance.

Me: Yes, you do. I've seen you. *(Takes left arm and lifts it.)* Just put your left hand on her shoulder, like this, and then, maybe touch the back of her hair with your other hand. *(Puts hand to back of head.)* Then pull her close to you . . .

Scott: Like this? *(Pulls me close, closes eyes, and . . . we kiss!)*

Me: *(Whispers.)* Perfect. *(Takes in breath. Opens eyes.)* Minus the mustache, of course. *(Straightens mustache.)*

Scott: *(Cracks up laughing.)*

Me: Was it . . . awful? The mustache, I mean.

Scott: Kind of like kissing Santa Claus.

Me: *(Playfully punches him in the arm.)* Thanks a lot, mister! Some Romeo. Sure, kiss me now, but kill me later.

Scott: No, seriously, thanks. It's good practice. *(Lowers voice.)* In case I'm ever in a play where I have to give mouth-to-mouth to a yeti.

Me: *(Cracks up.)* Thanks a lot. Now, go out there and knock 'em dead. But first, one more little piece of advice.

Scott: Yeah, great. What is it?

Me: Whatever you do, when you're about to kiss Jayden . . .

Scott: Yeah?

Me: Just picture a yeti!

Scott: *(Cracks up.)* A green-eyed yeti, you mean.

Me: Now go. Good luck! I mean, break a leg. *(Pushes Romeo through curtain onto stage. House lights dim.)*

Me: *(Steps into the wings backstage. Hands go to my lips—not to straighten my mustache this time. Sound disappears. Thinks. Remembers. To self: For just a moment, one perfect moment, I got to be Juliet.)*

Romeo and Juliet Math
by Joey Reel

- Number of kisses in Romeo and Juliet: At least 2
- Number of kisses there should be: 0 (unless they're seals)
- Number of people who die in a sword fight: 2
- Number of injuries in sword fights: 1, when Alex poked Scott Towel with cardboard tube
- Number of poisonings: 2
- Number of people Romeo murders, including himself: 3
- Number of times Romeo falls off balcony: 0
- Number of times Scott Towel falls off balcony: Too many to count
- Number of sonnets in Romeo and Juliet: 3½
- Number of times Shakespeare pops up if you Google him: 44 million
- Number of lines Romeo says: 617
- Number of lines Juliet says and Alex wishes she had: 542
- Number of lines Jayden says correctly: Not 542

In Reel Life

Upstairs in my room, I glued the final cloud pictures on my poster board, a series of almost-purple clouds from tonight's sunset. I was mopping up extra glue when Alex and Joey came back from the Raven. Alex, still half-dressed as Tybalt in boots, tights, and a long, puffy-sleeved shirt, floated across the room. She leaned against the bookcase as if she needed it to help hold her up.

"How was dress rehearsal?" I asked.

Joey circled around the rug, waving her arms. "You should have seen it, Stevie. Romeo climbed up Dad's ladder without falling for once, but his arm got caught on Jayden's belt, and the whole thing broke.

Hundreds of pearls went flying and Jayden was, like, 'Whoa,' and she slipped and fell right as Romeo was about to kiss Juliet."

"Don't look at me," Alex said with a glint in her eye.

"It was so funny, I died laughing. Except Mr. Cannon didn't think so. Dad asked me if I did it on purpose but I didn't. Cross my heart!"

"Joey, you couldn't have done better if you'd planned it," Alex said.

"Oh, man, I can't believe I missed it. Sorry about all your pearls, though, Duck. It took you, like, forever to string them."

"So? It was fun. Then Mercutio dropped his sword two times when he was sword-fighting Alex, and one time, his tights fell down!"

"Did the trap door work?" I asked.

"Yep," Joey said. "Dad was super psyched."

"I wish I could have come over. But I had to finish this cloud poster or it would ruin my whole weekend. I'll come to opening night, Alex, I promise."

"Alex made a super good Tybalt," said Joey. "Even though I still think she'd be the best Juliet."

"Alex? Earth to Alex," I said.

"Who, me? Oh, the play. I lived. I died. All in one night. It was . . . perfect."

I raised an eyebrow at Joey. Alex sure was in one of her good moods.

"Um, I have to go get out of this stage makeup," said Alex. "But . . . let's all get into our pj's and meet back here in five for a Sisters Club meeting."

Joey squealed. "Pajama jam!" I grabbed my pj's from under my pillow.

When Alex came back, all three of us sat cross-legged on the thick daisy-shaped rug, leaning against the beds. "Wait," I said dramatically, closing my eyes and holding my fingers to my temples. "Something is different here tonight. I think I'm getting a vibe." I held out one hand, pretending to touch the air around Joey's head. "Joey got rich tonight!"

"Wow! She's right!" said Joey. "Dad gave me twenty-five whole dollars for helping out so much making props and working on the sets." She glanced over at Alex. "How'd you do that, Stevie?" she said in a fake voice.

"And . . ." This time I patted the air around Alex.

"Hold on, hold on. I'm getting something. Alex. It's your aura. It's different."

"Is not."

"Is too!"

"Stevie, my *aura* is just fine, thank you very much."

"Go ahead, make fun, but thou dost protest too much." I felt the top of her head, picked up her hand and held it. "I'm seeing . . . a dark place. Behind a door. No, a curtain. I see . . . two boys. No, wait. One is a girl dressed as a boy. She has a mustache."

Alex pulled her hand away. Instinctively, she fingered her upper lip.

"And . . . here comes the good part . . . they kiss!"

"Uh! Stevie! How did you know that?" She grabbed one of Joey's stuffed animals and started clobbering me with it.

"Scott Towel really kissed you? Stevie must have ESP."

"Yeah. Extra *spying* powers," said Alex, looking around. "Where is it?"

"Where's what?"

"Okay, okay. I give." I grinned, holding up the baby monitor.

"You sneak!" said Alex. "I forgot all about that thing."

"I wanted to finish my cloud project, so I asked Joey to turn it on for me."

"You knew?" Alex said to Joey. "You little spy." She turned on Joey and launched a major tickle attack.

"So, Alex. Tell us about the Big Kiss. The amazing Scott Towel Smoocheroo."

"My lips are sealed." Alex mimed zipping her lips.

"Sealed with a kiss!" said Joey, and we all burst into fits of hysterics. "Just think, Alex," said Joey, "someday you could be Mrs. Paper Towel."

"Jo-ey!" Alex clobbered her this time.

"Wherefore art thou, Mr. Towel. Parting is such sweet sorrow," I teased.

"Fine. Go ahead. Make fun all you want, but at least I *finally* got my first kiss. It's so humiliating that my little sister beat me to it by two whole weeks."

"You know, if you think about it, that wasn't really Stevie's first kiss anyway," Joey pointed out.

"What do you mean it wasn't my first kiss?" I asked.

"You already had your first kiss. By Scott Towel. That time, in the play, when you filled in for Alex in *Beauty and the Beast*."

"Way to make me feel better, Joey," said Alex.

"I got my first kiss, too," said Joey.

"Huh? What?" Alex and I said at the same time, gaping at Joey.

"You? You're only eight!" said Alex.

"Nine."

"Who kissed you?" I asked.

"Scott Towel. On the ear. Remember that time he came for dinner and I knocked his fork into the fondue pot and he tried to hide under the table?"

"I forgot about that!" I said. "You called him Frog Lips. And you tried to wipe off the boy cooties for, like, a week."

"Perfect. So everyone on the planet got kissed by Frog Lips before I did."

Alex leaned her head back against the bed, clutching the drama-masks necklace she always wore. I wondered if she was still thinking about the kiss. "I guess we'll just have to change the Sisters Club to the Kissers Club now."

I expected Joey to yell "Gross" and go on about boy cooties and ask us why couldn't it just stay the way it was. But she didn't.

Instead, she laughed and said, "But you know, we can still have 'Sisters, Blisters, and Tongue Twisters' for our motto, because Alex said a tongue twister is another name for a kiss."

"Speaking of Sisters Club," I said, "I have an idea. For what we can do for our meeting. Starting right now."

"Do we have to burn stuff again?" Joey asked.

"No. Listen. Hear me out. I say we play Truth or Dare and Alex has to go first because she always picks truth."

"I pick dare sometimes," Alex argued.

"When?" Joey and I said at the same time.

"Okay, but you guys both have to play too."

"No way," said Joey. "Smart people don't take dares."

"C'mon, Duck," I pleaded. "Don't be a Mary Sue. It's not scary dares. Just funny ones. Alex goes first. Truth or dare?"

She pretended to think it over.

"Truth," she said. "But you can't ask me anything about Scott Howell. A.k.a. Romeo." She held her hands to her chest.

I asked her anyway. "What was it like? Your first kiss. With Scott Towel."

"Gross," said Joey. "This is boring."

"Don't worry, Joey. I'm not telling anyway. It's personal."

"C'mon, Alex. You know you want to. You're just going to tell Sock Monkey anyway, and we're going to listen."

"Not me," said Joey.

"Ask me something else," said Alex.

"What did you *really* wish the day we threw stuff into the fire?" I asked.

"Why do you have that shirt with a swear in your drawer?" Joey said.

"What! I don't have—what shirt?"

"You know, the shirt you wear that makes you *itch,*" Joey said.

"Or act like a *snitch,*" I added, picking up on Joey's lead.

"Or want to get *rich,*" Joey said with a snort. "Or

look like an *ostrich.*" She was rolling on the floor with laughter.

"Or feel like a *witch,*" I said.

"What is this, National Poetry Week? Wait a second. I get it. How do you guys know about that?"

"Stevie was snooping," Joey accused me, pointing.

"Nah-uh! Her frog got lost and—" Joey shot me a look. "Never mind."

"No fair, anyway. That's *two* questions," said Alex.

"If you answer both questions," I offered, "you get to call the truths or dares for Joey and me."

"Deal," said Alex.

"The truth!" I reminded her.

"First, Joey's question. I went to this sleepover, right? We played this weird game where you had to take off one thing you're wearing and pass it to the person on your right. I gave up my favorite braided bracelet, the one with the little heart charm? And I got stuck with that shirt. I don't even know the girl. So, I didn't know if it was a joke or what."

"But you kept it!" said Joey. "If Mom finds out, she'll freak!"

"I didn't want everyone to think I was a baby, so I

tried to act like it was cool. As soon as I got home, I stuffed it in the bottom of my drawer."

"What are you going to do with it?"

"I don't know. I can't exactly wear it to school. But maybe I could wear it sometime to a basketball game or a party or something."

"Yeah, wear it to a weird party where you play that weird game again and give it to somebody else."

Alex looked Joey in the eye. "So, Joey. You can't tell, okay? This is a sisters thing. Promise?" Joey nodded.

"And Stevie? You're right. I didn't wish I'd get the part of Juliet the night of the storm. I wished I'd get my first kiss from Scott. And it came true! Like magic!"

"My wish came true for somebody else," said Joey.

"What was your wish?" I asked.

"I wished I could see a blue frog. Then some people near here in Oregon found a rare blue frog in their backyard. I saw it on the news."

"So you did see a blue frog . . . on TV," said Alex. "That still counts."

"But guess what? That's not all. They're going to

be bringing it around to schools around here to show kids, so my wish *is* going to come true!"

I thought back to the night of the storm, and how making a wish in the fire seemed like a long time ago. I'd wished for something new and exciting and different to happen. Daring, even. Making friends with a boy was new and different. And growing up sure was turning out to be more exciting than I thought. Daring? Just daring to be myself was enough. For now.

"Stevie's turn!" said Joey. "I know! Make her go outside in her pajamas and act like a gorilla for one minute. Or sing and act out 'I'm a Little Teapot.'"

"Look who's all over this game now," I remarked. "Little Miss I'm Too Smart for Dares." Joey stuck out her tongue at me like a frog.

"Go outside in your pajamas and do the Hokey Pokey," said Joey.

"That's a good one," said Alex. "But I get to call it."

"You didn't even say 'truth or dare' yet!"

"Truth or dare?" Joey yelled.

"Truth," I answered.

"Truth, huh?" said Alex, rubbing her hands together.

"So, my question is . . . what I want to ask is . . . Did you ever let that Wire Rims guy kiss you? You know, after that day you fell in the pool?"

"His name's Owen," I said.

"Well, did you? You have to answer the question."

"No!" I said. Truthfully.

We had been hanging out a bunch these past couple of weeks — in the name of Science, of course. We were still trying to make a cloud form and get a picture of it. So far, we could have filled a scrapbook with failed attempts.

"This is *so* not about Science," Olivia kept teasing me whenever she got the chance.

Deep down, I guess Olivia was right. There was a small part of me that liked that Owen liked me. But I knew I was a little afraid of it, too. Being Science buddies, and friends, felt right. For now.

Time to change the subject. "Joey. Truth or dare?" I asked.

"Dare," Joey said bravely.

Alex glanced around, searching for an idea. "Your dare, Joey Reel, should you choose to accept it, but you have to, is . . . you have to kiss Sir Croaks-a-Lot!"

"What's so bad about that? I'll kiss a frog."

"Really?" asked Alex.

"Really?" I asked.

"Watch me!" Joey went over to the tank on her desk and scooped up her frog. She held him in her hand, with just his head peeking out of her fist. Then, she planted a kiss right on his head, warts and all.

"See?" she said proudly.

"Wow. You didn't turn into a toad or anything," I said. "But, ooh, you do have a wart growing right here." I pointed to my cheek.

"And here," said Alex, indicating her forehead.

Joey ran to the mirror. "You guys!" she screeched. Alex and I rolled on the floor with laughter.

"Sleep here tonight?" Joey asked Alex. "In our room?" But she didn't need to ask. Alex was already stretched out on the floor between us, bundled like a newborn in her favorite blanket, half-asleep.

I clicked off the light, but before crawling under the covers, I pressed my face to the window, peering out past the old tulip tree.

Outside, the dark had deepened, but there was a moon and clouds, and no wind was howling. No thunder, no lightning. Just three sisters, warm and cozy, wrapped in fuzzy blankets like we could weather any storm.

Storms would come and storms would go. Boys would come and boys would go.

But sisters are forever.

How much I L